They had to get out of the blizzard.

"We'll need to listen for the snowmobile," said Rain. "I think the guy with the gun is looking for the summit pass."

"He's been out here in a storm for an hour and hasn't given up." That level of persistence didn't sit well with David.

"We're much better at navigating these woods than he is," she said, so matter-of-factly. But that's how she'd always been. Seeing Rain was dragging up all kinds of feelings, and after the way she'd abruptly broken off their relationship, there was no way he could trust himself with those feelings. But that was the past, so he'd focus on what was in front of him.

"He'll run out of gas if he doesn't head home soon," Rain said. She looked out into the valley, hidden in a cloak of white.

It was a good point, but if their pursuer retreated, that would only give them temporary reprieve. He'd deal with that later... For now, they needed to get going before it got dark.

Rebecca Hopewell is the kiss-only pen name for an award-winning romance author. In addition to writing, she loves to read, wander in the forest and talk with friends and family. A perfect day is when she manages to do all four of these things! Rebecca lives just outside San Francisco.

High-Stakes Blizzard

REBECCA HOPEWELL

LOVE INSPIRED
INSPIRATIONAL ROMANCE

LOVE INSPIRED®

INSPIRATIONAL ROMANCE

ISBN-13: 978-1-335-55597-7

High-Stakes Blizzard

Copyright © 2023 by Rebecca Hopewell

For questions and comments about the quality of this book, please contact us
at CustomerService@Harlequin.com.

Love Inspired
22 Adelaide St. West, 41st Floor
Toronto, Ontario M5H 4E3, Canada
www.LoveInspired.com

Printed in U.S.A.

Recycling programs
for this product may
not exist in your area.

Let not mercy and truth forsake thee: bind them about thy neck; write them upon the table of thine heart.
—*Proverbs* 3:3

To Wendy Musell, for your support and enthusiasm all along but especially in the early stages of this book. Our discussion on the many considerations when writing this book was invaluable.

And to Gabriela Kramer, for countless talks about our mutual love of romance and that one walk where we discussed triage techniques. I hope I properly saved my character's life.

P.S. You both do amazing work!

Chapter One

Rain Jordan belonged in the mountains. She thrived in their complicated beauty, their indomitable obstacles. It was the place she found it easiest to believe that the world made sense.

The landscape in front of her was covered in a blanket of snow, with granite boulders and clumps of evergreens jutting out of the frozen landscape. Even if she couldn't see the path, Rain knew how to navigate this mountain, between boulders and through stands of trees, up to the ridge. She snowshoed through the white drifts, and Maple followed in the path of her footprints, her paws sinking into the snow with each playful jump. The snow muted the rustle of the trees and the buzz of a snowmobile in the distance. The loudest sounds were her own breaths and the scrape of her jacket and snow pants each time she took a step.

"Getting tired, girl?" she said over her shoulder.

Maple panted back at her, wagging her tail. The German shepherd she'd inherited from her brother, Brandon, seemed to thrive out here in the wilderness just as much as Rain did.

These woods used to be her second home. During the summers, Rain, Brandon and their parents had walked every trail, exploring every edible plant, every mountain stream, every shelter option. During the winters, they'd follow the animal tracks, making their way through the snow-topped trees—sometimes on skis, sometimes on snowshoes—to see the endless views of the Tahoe Wilderness cloaked in white. The mountains held secrets, hidden away from the world but there for anyone who ventured in. For those who knew where to look.

But all those memories were clouded by the night a drunk driver had collided with her parents' car when Rain was eighteen, leaving her and her older brother alone. Only the forest and their cabin on Crystal Lake tied them to their childhood. It had never been enough. The emptiness that night had left lingered inside her, heavy and hollow.

In the first year after their parents' deaths, Rain had worried about how defeated Brandon had seemed as the bills piled up. First they'd sold their parents' house, but the second mortgage on it meant they'd barely broken even. Then Brandon floated the idea of selling their cabin, but she'd put her foot down. There *had* to be another way. They'd argued until he dropped the subject. But he'd gotten more secretive, and when she'd tried to talk to him about the money, he'd said he had a solution. She'd tried to trust him, but more than once, she'd caught him looking over his shoulder when they were out, like he suspected someone was watching him. Now Brandon was gone, too.

Rain continued up the snowy mountain, thinking about all the reasons her brother had come up this path to the ridge seven months ago. Maybe it was a sentimental whim, or maybe he'd had a plan. Her brother always had plans. But why hadn't he taken Maple with him? The dog followed him everywhere when they were at their cabin. Even harder to understand was how he could have fallen from the ridge and disappeared from her life forever. He knew the mountain even better than she did, and she'd never make this mistake.

But after seven months, Rain was done asking these questions. She had to accept God's plan for her. She really wanted to, but when so much had gone wrong, doing so was hard. Still, she'd inherited Maple, a ray of light in all the darkness. It was time to make peace with Brandon's death.

Rain looked up at the dark, heavy clouds blowing in from the north. A storm was coming, and the news had predicted up to three more feet of new snow during the next two days. She'd told herself that was why she'd dumped her bags in the front hall when she arrived and headed out immediately, without even taking off her boots—she wanted to beat the storm. But that wasn't the whole truth. Even after seven months, it was still painful to face her family cabin alone. All the memories this cabin held were now hers alone.

But she was ready to face the place again... At least, she hoped she was, especially since the blizzard was predicted to blanket the Sierra Nevadas. It would bury the road, and the plows wouldn't make their way up to Crystal Lake for days, leaving the handful of cabins in the area stranded. But the cabin was always stocked with extra supplies of food, propane and firewood, and if she needed anything, she'd seen David Hernandez's search and rescue truck at his family's cabin on her drive in. Not that going over there was a good option. Rain swallowed the inevitable rush of feelings that came when that name went through her mind. David Hernandez was no longer part of her life, and there was no use thinking about the past.

Instead, Rain focused on the blue sky disappearing between the clouds and the ridge where her brother had fallen. She was ready to crest the ridge, find a way to say goodbye and move forward, even though it meant she and Maple would be spending this week alone, snowed in.

After a few hundred feet of climbing, Rain neared the highest lookout that was accessible without climbing gear. The trail ended along a narrow ridge overlooking the valley of trees and rocky peaks. Crystal Ridge, their family had called it, though the name probably wasn't official. In the distance, the little town of Clover Valley peeked through the evergreens, with the gas station at one end, the general store rising up in the middle and the little urgent care center at the other end. She took a few more steps, then stopped. Why had her brother come here, then walked too close to the edge? It was a mystery, but she was letting that go, too.

She took a step toward the precipice, where Brandon had fallen. It was time. She unzipped her pocket and pulled out a letter she'd written to him the first time he'd run away, many years ago. She kissed the carefully folded paper and let the wind take it away.

"Goodbye," she whispered as it floated out into the snowy air.

She had expected to feel different in that moment, to get some sort of relief, but she felt the same. Maybe even emptier. Rain frowned and took another step. Maple nosed her hand in warning.

"It's okay, girl," she said, stroking the dog's muzzle. "I'm not going any closer."

Rain gazed down at the rocky ledge where her brother had landed, twenty yards or so below. It was their cookout ledge. During those summers years ago, she, Brandon, David and his sister, Isabel, had trekked over the summit, following the base of the granite peaks so they could cook out on that landing. The path up to that ledge was hidden between large boulders. The place had always felt like it was just theirs, a cove protected from the wind by the stand of white firs on one side and one of the deep caves that ran under the summit on the other. If only there had been early snow, his fall might have been cushioned. If only Brandon had fallen a few yards over, one of the enormous firs might have broken—

The sharp sound of a snowmobile's motor broke into her thoughts. It buzzed loudly and then cut out. Someone was close. Another gust of wind blew up the mountainside, and Maple let out a low growl. During the seven months they'd been together, Rain had never heard Maple growl. Ever. She turned and scanned the trail behind them, where the dog was aiming her warning, but nothing appeared. One quick glance at her phone made her heart kick up in her chest: from where she was standing, she was out of cell range.

When she looked up again, a man stepped out from behind the granite wall of the summit, his boots sinking into the deep snow. Rain sized him up: a black hat, reflective ski goggles, black snow pants and a black coat with a bright blue insignia on the breast she couldn't quite make out. Something about the way he seemed to silently focus on her felt menacing. He wasn't wearing snowshoes, so at least she could move faster than he could on foot. When he got back on his snowmobile, he had the upper hand by far. The man's gaze darted between her and Maple. He slowly approached them, then came to a stop a few yards away. Maple was close and on high alert, tail down, and another low growl escaped through her teeth.

"Stay," she said quietly.

"Brandon's sister, right? Rain." It sounded more like a statement than a question, and Rain's heart gave a startled thud. Why did this man know who she was? "He said the shipment was up here at your cabin, but we've searched everywhere. I knew you'd come back for it, sooner or later."

Rain's heart pounded in her chest. What was he talking about? Her instincts were telling her to run, but how was she supposed to escape on foot from a man on a snowmobile? Then there was the part of her that had wondered about her brother's death for the past seven months. That part of her wasn't ready to run away yet. Maybe she had been right all along. Brandon's death hadn't been an accident. Her heart jumped at the possibility that she might find the answers she was searching for.

Rain kept her expression neutral and returned the man's steady gaze. "What do you know about my brother?"

The guy ignored her question. "I'm here to make you a deal. We're willing to give you the same price, even though you didn't bring them over the Nevada line."

We? Bring them over the Nevada line? Fear pumped through her as these words sunk in. She had tried so hard not to assume the worst, but these ominous words suggested Brandon had gotten into something bad. What was it?

The man took a step toward her, and a chill ran through her body as she raced to piece together the situation. He'd been watching her, waiting for her. He thought she had something he needed. Rain pushed away her fear, trying to figure out her next move.

Maple growled louder this time, and the man pulled out a gun from inside his jacket. "I'll shoot that dog if I need to."

Rain's breath caught in her throat as she stared at his gun. No. She couldn't lose Maple. She had lost too much already.

"Go home, Maple," she said, pointing to the path down the mountain. "Go to the cabin."

The dog didn't move, just looked up at her, her eyes dark and attentive. Rain pleaded with her gaze. *You can't get hurt. You're all I have left.*

"Go on," she said, trying not to let her voice shake. "I'll be there soon."

Maple eyed her warily, then started back along the path, passing the man with her teeth bared, until she disappeared behind the granite wall. Rain took a steadying breath. What was her next move? The snow was deep enough that she'd be able to outmaneuver the guy in her snowshoes, but he had a gun and a snowmobile, making that option moot. Either she had to figure out how to disarm this guy, or she had to find a way to escape. Quickly. Behind her was the end of the path, and to one side was the summit rock. On the other side was the cliff. Rain took a step back.

"Stop." His voice was louder, angrier. "You're not going anywhere. Where are they?"

Her breath caught in her throat. Everything he'd said made her suspect he was involved in Brandon's death. The rigid jaw, the sharpness of his voice, the gun he gripped—it all suggested he wouldn't hesitate to use violence on her.

The man must have read the fear on her face. "All you have to do is tell me where they are."

"I don't know what you're talking about." Desperation seeped into her voice. "I don't even know who you are. So we can both just walk away."

The man shook his head. "Not a chance. Your brother screwed us over. We need that other half of our stash, and you're going to get it for us."

"But I don't know where it is."

The man didn't answer, and she was pretty sure he didn't believe her. It occurred to Rain that he'd likely been waiting for this moment since Brandon died. If he got hold of her, she was almost sure that this would end disastrously.

Rain glanced down the sheer drop off the edge of the ridge again. She was *not* going to die the same way Brandon did. She eyed the tall firs below, covered with snow, the ones she'd wished her brother had fallen into. They were her only chance. She couldn't wait for this man to catch her off guard. She had to willingly jump to make it those few extra feet if she had any hope of hitting them.

Can I make myself jump?

She took a step toward the ledge. Another.

The man raised his gun, pointing it at her. "I'm not letting this go."

Please, God, help me get this right.

Rain took a deep breath. She turned to the edge, focusing on the tips of the firs, and forced herself to jump out as far as she could.

Her mind went blank as her body dropped through the cold air, the tree whizzing toward her until she hit it. Needles scraped her face as she grasped for the branches that slipped through her gloves. She tumbled, bouncing forward into another tree. Limbs cracked as she hit them with her shins, her back, her stomach. One of her snowshoes twisted, and the other caught, suspending her for a moment before it released with a sharp snap. A mess of green and brown and white was falling everywhere around her. Her thoughts kicked in at the last minute, and she remembered to curl up and tuck her head.

Rain hit the snowy ground with a hard thud that took her breath away. Branches and clumps of snow from the trees followed, covering her. She scrambled to move, caught under a tree limb as more snow buried her. She clawed at the heavy load, struggling to orient herself. Getting her feet under her, then her knees, she dug desperately with her hands, her heart pounding in her chest.

Help me, Lord.

She pushed up with one foot, moving the snow out of the way in this tiny cave that had formed, until she broke through. The cold wind came rushing in. She had made it. She was alive. Thank God. Rain patted herself down, checking for injuries. Her ribs were sore but okay, and she could move the arm she had fallen on without pain. Both snowshoes were gone, and one ankle was throbbing, but her pack was still on her back. She'd escaped and survived...so far.

Rain looked up between the trees and saw the man staring down at her. He knew she was alive. He looked around, like he was assessing how to get to where she was.

"I'll find you," he called down to her. "You have until noon tomorrow to settle this with me, or..."

He let the words hang in the air, then turned around and disappeared. What would he do if he didn't get what he was looking for? The thought of Maple waiting for her at the cabin gave her a new jolt of fear. She heard the whiny buzz of the snowmobile again. Was he still coming for her?

If you know how to be invisible in the forest, you have time. Her father's voice was a balm, a reminder to wait, to take her time, and Rain had just bought herself a little more of that time. This side of the mountain was much steeper and less accessible on a snowmobile, especially for someone unfamiliar with the terrain, and the path to their cookout ledge was almost impossible to find. But snow was starting to fall. The storm was coming in, bringing wind and a few more feet of snow. How could she make it back to her cabin with a twisted ankle and no snowshoes?

After the rush of adrenaline from these last minutes, her body was shutting down. Rain knew all the signs, but she was tired, so tired, and for just one long moment, she wanted to lie back in the snow and go to sleep, despite all the dangers. But when she closed her eyes she saw Maple, sitting on the porch of the cabin. Rain was all that Maple had. If she didn't find her way back, her dog would spend the night outside, waiting...or worse. She wouldn't make it in these temperatures.

The buzz of the snowmobile grew louder, then dimmed again. How long did she have before he found her? She was on the other side of the mountain now, and even if he crossed the summit pass, the entrance path to the cookout ledge was hard to find. But the man had a snowmobile, which gave him speed, and though the mountain was steep on this side, if he found the entrance he'd trap her here. That would force her into the caves, which were far too small for her comfort.

Rain took a deep breath and wrestled the pack off her back, then unzipped it clumsily, unwilling to take off her gloves and expose her hands. First, she needed energy. Rain unscrewed the thermos cap and took a long gulp of hot chocolate. The warmth trailed down her throat, spreading through her body. She reached in the bag for a few handfuls of trail mix and washed them down with another drink of hot chocolate. She rested her injured ankle on a branch, slightly elevated, and took a deep, calming breath. *Think through the pain. Take your time.* Memories of her father's soothing voice whispered to her through the trees.

She had a phone with her, but the chances of reception were slim…if the cell towers were still working. She couldn't count on that in a storm. Even if she did reach 911, and even on the off chance someone on the team knew this area of the wilderness enough to find her, they wouldn't make it up here before the storm. Crystal Lake was too high up the mountain, too far away from town.

But there was someone else close by. Someone who knew this mountain just as well as she did. David Hernandez. As much as it would hurt to call him, hurt to hear his voice again, she knew he would come, despite the danger. Despite the ways she'd caused him pain. He couldn't help it—that was just who he was. She knew this part of him so well. After all, it was why she had ended their engagement all those years ago.

Calling him could put him in danger. But snowmobiles were clumsy, announcing their arrival for miles. And if she warned David, he could stay out of sight of the man with the gun. Of course, this was all assuming he'd answer her call.

She pawed around for her phone and looked for the reception. One little bar flickered in the top corner. Quickly, she scrolled through her contacts until she found the one she should have deleted five years ago. She pressed it and waited. After a few long moments of silence, the call connected.

"Rain?" He sounded confused, which was fair. They hadn't talked since the day she'd returned the ring.

She pushed away all the memories his voice threatened to unearth.

"Yes, it's me," she said, making sure her voice didn't shake. "Please. I need your help."

David Hernandez's skis slid through the snow, making parallel tracks behind the path of the rescue sled he was pushing. The road was covered in a fresh layer of powder, and more was coming down quickly, covering the orange rescue bag and the first aid pack. He was hoping he didn't have to use either of these items, but from the few words he'd heard

through the phone from Rain before the call dropped off entirely, it didn't look good.

"Our old cookout ledge…my ankle…maple coming…man with a gun."

Only one of those snips of information was clear, the cookout ledge. The mention of her ankle left him wondering if she was hurt. He had no idea what to do with the third phrase he'd heard. Did maples even grow at this elevation? With each stride, he turned the words *maple coming*, over in his mind, mostly so that he didn't think about the last thing she'd said. *A man with a gun.* His entire body had frozen when he heard those words.

David was used to danger, and he worked well in frightening situations. It was why he'd become a firefighter: he was willing to do whatever it took to save lives. It wasn't that he was fearless. He had a healthy amount of fear, which had saved him dozens of times. It was just that, in the face of fear, his instinct was to act. But when Rain spoke those words, for the first time he could remember, fear threatened to overwhelm him. *What if I can't help Rain in time?*

So he had left his sister back at the cabin without much explanation except that he needed to make a rescue. Isabel was used to that. David already had used the rescue sled twice this winter on his days off. He hoped this wouldn't be his third. He didn't tell Isabel that Rain had been on the other end of the phone call, because he didn't need to hear his sister's warnings. They were already clanging in his head the moment he picked up the call.

You can't trust her.

The sky was dumping snow as he turned off the road to the buried trail that led up the mountain. The wind was starting to pick up, which meant visibility was going down. Someone was up there with a snowmobile, which didn't strike David as a great idea, considering the conditions. Then again, he was heading up the mountain on skis to rescue the woman who had left him, so he wasn't anyone to judge.

David pushed the sled up the hill formed by the snowplow. As he turned, he caught movement out of the corner of his eye. He froze, Rain's warning about a man with a gun ringing in his ears. He scanned the blurry white landscape and spotted...a dog? It was a big one, a German shepherd, mostly brown with just a little black around the face, and it was hopping through the snow, toward him. Strange. Who would let a dog wander around in this weather? Was it lost? There were only a few cabins out here, most of them on the other side of Crystal Lake, and the campground was buried in the snow.

The dog came closer. Its tail wasn't wagging, but it was up, like it was curious. David took off his glove and put his hand out, and the dog came closer and sniffed it, then gave it a little nuzzle. The dog seemed to be happy to see him. At any other time, he'd turn back and take it home, but Rain needed help.

"Sorry, buddy," he said, stroking the dog's head. "I'd help you out, but I need to go."

He unsnapped his pocket and stuffed his hand inside, pulling out his various food options. Peanuts? No. Maybe the dried jerky his neighbor had made… David wasn't sure if this qualified as dog food, but a dog out in a snowstorm wouldn't survive long, so he decided to risk it. He dug some jerky out of the bag, and the dog gobbled it up, so he gave it a little more.

"I really have to go," he said, scratching the dog under its collar. The collar. This dog probably had tags with its owner's number on it. He scratched the dog's neck again, then reached around to pull up the buckle side of the collar. He turned over the silver charm in his glove.

Maple.

The word he'd heard on the phone made sense. Maple wasn't a tree he was supposed to look for. It was a dog out wandering, missing its owner. Rain's dog. It must be. How had it found its way out here on its own when Rain was on the other side of the summit? He couldn't leave it behind. Maybe Maple could even help him find Rain.

David skied up to the sled and patted the orange insolated layer strapped on top.

"Hey, Maple. Come on up." The dog wagged her tail at the sound of her name and hopped onto the sled. So far, so good. "Lie down."

Maple settled on the orange blanket, facing David. Good enough.

David started up the covered mountain path, pushing the sled. The dog was welcome resistance as he made the uphill climb. Physical exercise helped settle him in urgent situations, letting him think. Besides, with the amount of work he had in front of him, the cold was better than the heat. During the summers, he and his team carried heavy packs through the blazing heat of the California summers to fight the forest fires that had been running rampant in the West in recent years.

They moved up the switchback path as the noise of the snowmobile grew louder, somewhere out of sight. Just after they passed the place where the buried path split, Maple jumped off the sled and headed the wrong way, toward Crystal Ridge. The prints all went in that direction, too.

"Where are you going, Maple?" he called.

The dog stopped and looked over its shoulder but didn't turn around.

Rain had referred to the old cookout ledge, but Maple wanted to follow a different path. Though the ridge was above the cookout ledge, both were accessed from opposite sides of the summit's tall, granite peaks. Strange. David was under the impression dogs had a knack for tracking. Did Maple get this wrong, or did the dog know more than he did? Either he trusted this dog's instincts, or he trusted what he'd heard from Rain.

"I have to try this way first. But I hear you. I'll keep that route in mind." David gave a wry laugh at his effort to explain it all to a dog who had no idea what he was saying. He tried again. "Come here. Let's get Rain."

Maple looked up the trail one more time, then back at him. Finally, the dog turned around and came to the sled.

"Good girl...or boy," he said, offering her some more jerky. The dog gobbled it up.

The wind was picking up as he climbed the last stretch, and the closer he got to the summit ridge, the harder it was to see where he was going. As he worked his way up, he searched for reasons why Maple might have wanted to go toward the ridge. Maybe Rain had taken that path first. After all, her brother had died falling from that ridge. The idea of her up there alone, looking down, made his gut twist. Just because their relationship had ended badly didn't mean the feelings just stopped. They lingered, coming out at unexpected times.

The wind lashed his exposed skin as they reached the summit pass, the sheer granite face rising up on one side, the precipitous drop on the other. It was narrow and icy, so he stuck close to the granite wall, following the animal tracks that poked through the deep snow. The wind was strongest up here, whipping fat flakes at his cheeks as he continued along the pass and down the other side, searching for signs of the entrance to the cookout ledge. It looked like another of the many caves, the entrance formed by two boulders, but a step into the crevice revealed an opening to the ledge, sheltered from the wind. It was their own little cove, or at least it had been all those years ago. He continued down, sticking as close to the cliffs as he could. Too close and he'd get lost in the wrong jumble of boulders, but too far and he'd miss the entrance entirely. David slowed the sled, scanning the mountain through the blowing snow. Finally, he spotted the familiar double pines that stood just before the entrance. He pushed aside all the memories that this place threatened to bring back and steered the sled toward the cave. There was a dusting of snow in the passage, just enough to cushion the sled. Maple's ears perked as they entered, and she started to get up.

"Stay," he said. "We're almost there."

The dog turned around on the sled but stayed on. He pushed the sled up the bank of snow onto the ledge. He'd made it. David headed straight for the entrance to the low cave in the middle. They'd escaped a storm in there more than once, so he'd assumed Rain would take shelter here. He peered in, but it was empty.

"Rain? Where are you?" His voice didn't travel far in this wind.

David's fear came back with a vengeance. He

looked around for tracks, but the snow was pristine, untouched. Something was wrong. Had the man with the gun found her before she made it to the ledge?

"Rain?" He could hear a hint of desperation in his voice. How was he supposed to find her? *Please, God, let her be okay.* David hadn't prayed in years, but the words came to him anyway.

His heart leaped as Maple jumped off the sled and headed for the trees ahead, bounding through the deep snow. The dog disappeared in between them.

"Maple?"

She didn't come, so he followed the dog's tracks, leading into the trees. He left his sled and continued, brushing the branches out of his way.

In front of him, he found Rain in a cocoon of snow and branches, and Maple was in it, too, licking her face.

"David. You came." Rain looked up and gave him a smile that took his breath away. "And you found Maple, too."

Chapter Two

Maple yelped and licked Rain's cheek, then tried to climb onto her lap, almost knocking her back into the snow.

"Take it easy, girl," Rain said, stroking the dog behind her ears. "Settle down."

It was as much advice for herself as it was for Maple. Rain's heart was racing in her chest. It had taken off the moment Maple stepped through the trees, then jumped when David appeared. Now he was looking at her with those dark brown eyes she'd never forgotten.

David really was here.

Their call had cut off at some point, and when she'd tried to call him back, the signal she'd found just moments before was gone. She'd had no idea if he'd even heard where she was or if the man on the snowmobile would follow him or if...

She'd tried to block out her worries by focusing

on the immediate concerns: keeping warm and keeping out of sight. To keep herself warm and focused, she'd crawled around in the drifts of snow and gathered the fallen branches that had snapped off during her descent from the Crystal Ridge. Careful to stay off her ankle, she'd piled them haphazardly around the little hole her body had made in the snow, building it up so she wasn't visible from the ridge. The snowmobile had stopped a second time on the ridge above her, so she curled up and waited. A few moments later, the engine had started again.

The storm had picked up, covering her in a fluffy layer as she sat, waiting. The longer she sat there, the less her ankle throbbed, though the pain didn't go away. The longer she waited, the harder it was not to lose hope. She was trying not to think about all the ways this could end badly for Maple. And for David. She'd asked her ex-fiancé to go up the mountain in a blizzard, where a man with a gun was hunting her. She hadn't fully thought that part through when she called, and when she checked her phone for service again, there was none. It was too late to take it back.

But David was here, looking down at her, covered in snow but alive and well. He didn't look angry, even though she'd had no right to call him. He was assessing her, and those familiar eyes were filled with concern. He wore his hair shorter now, which made his cheekbones stand out even more, but his lips looked just as soft and full. His shoulders were broader now, probably from years of keeping in top shape for his job. She told herself that the warmth she felt as he stood in front of her was relief. His gaze lingered on her cheek.

"Are you hurt?" he asked softly. "Your face is…"

Rain touched a tender spot on her cheek, then shook her head. "It's mostly my ankle that's a little sore. It got twisted in the fall but—"

"The fall?" His voice was quiet, controlled, but his eyes were sharp, searching hers.

She glanced over her shoulder at the ridge above them, the sheer wall of granite she had somehow made herself jump from. It was hard to believe she'd done it.

"I was on the ridge, trying to say goodbye to Brandon, but the man on the snowmobile came. He started for me, so…well, I jumped for these trees."

"You jumped." The words came out slow and tight. David looked up at the ridge, high above, then closed his eyes. When he opened them again, Rain couldn't read his expression.

"I didn't have another good option," she added.

He shut his eyes again, this time shaking his head. Emotions rolled off him, but she didn't know what they were. Frustration that she'd gotten herself into this mess? Maybe. But his thoughts weren't her business anymore. They hadn't been for five years.

David was frowning at her. "I only caught a little of your call, but I heard the man with the gun part."

"It's the man on the snowmobile." Rain paused, listening to the engine whining through the forest. "Did he see you?"

"I don't think so." He paused, then pointed to her boots. "You came in those?"

"I had snowshoes." She gestured to the heaps of snow behind her. "They're buried somewhere in there, and I'm pretty sure they're broken."

"You'll need to ride on my rescue sled to make it through the snow before night falls."

His rescue sled. Now she understood how Maple had made it through the deep snow. It was hard enough that she'd asked for emergency help from the man she left. Ride on his rescue sled while he pushed it uphill to the summit pass?

"You shouldn't push me," she said, pleading with her eyes for him to understand.

He either didn't notice or ignored her plea. "Maple had no complaints."

Maple had settled over Rain's lap, but at the sound of her name, she perked up.

"You know what I mean." Rain searched for a reason that might convince him. "You can't use all your energy like that. We don't know how long we'll be out there."

David frowned, and she was pretty sure he understood her point, even if he didn't like it. The slope from here to the summit pass was steep and treacherous, and the snow was coming down harder. Though she'd stuffed her usual snacks and first aid supplies into her pack, she only had planned to be out for an hour, maybe two. If everything went well, they'd be back at their cabins within a couple of hours, but if the man on the snowmobile was waiting at the summit for them, they could be out a lot longer. And with her ankle still aching, they needed to maximize their energy.

"How did you think you would get back?" he asked.

"I asked you to bring a pair of snowshoes or skis."

He raised his eyebrows. "I didn't get that part of the message."

"I'll be fine if I walk in your tracks," she said. He started to shake his head, so she added, "Just until we get to the summit pass."

The incline was steep, but it wasn't too far, at least not compared to the journey they'd have on the other side. She waited, and finally he nodded. He took off his skis, letting his feet sink into the deep snow. He took the laborious steps toward her, then reached out a hand, offering to help her up. She hesitated, then nudged Maple until the dog wriggled off. Rain took a deep breath and placed her glove in David's. He helped her to standing, and somehow this simple gesture had her heart thumping again.

She ignored that sensation and focused on testing her weight on her ankle. So far, so good. She moved it experimentally to one side, then the other... Ouch.

Still painful. She needed to be careful not to roll it while she walked.

Rain lifted her gaze to find David watching her with a look she couldn't read. She searched for something to say. "Thank you for being here. I can't believe you came."

She'd meant that last sentence as a joke, but he didn't smile. He just looked at her with those dark, serious eyes.

"Neither can I."

The rescue sled was already covered with snow by the time David came out of the little clump of trees. He tipped off the new layer of white and turned it around, trying to keep an eye on Rain without looking like he was studying her. Did he catch a wince when she put her weight on her left foot? He was trying so hard not to think about her fall from the ridge and all the ways it could have gone terribly wrong. David had given up praying years ago, back when his best friend died in that terrible fire that almost took David, too. Now the words came to him like they had been there all this time.

Thank You, Lord, for keeping Rain safe.

He wasn't ready to think any more about the feelings that seeing Rain was dragging up, but it was hard not to notice the differences since the last time he'd seen her. Her brown hair peeked out from under her winter hat, shorter, more practical for her job, he suspected, and her brown eyes looked tired, like the years had weighed heavily on her. He frowned at the way those little details tugged at his emotions. After she'd so abruptly broken off their relationship and the friendship they'd had for even longer, he could not trust himself to let in those feelings. And after the way he'd accused her of being selfish that last day, he was sure she was thinking the same thing. But that was the past, so he put it aside and focused on what was in front of him. The three of them had to get out of the blizzard.

"We'll need to listen for the snowmobile," said Rain. "I think the guy is looking for the summit pass."

"He's been out there for an hour in a blizzard, and he hasn't given up." That level of persistence wasn't sitting well with David.

"We're much better at navigating these woods than he is," she said, so matter-of-factly. But that was always how she had been. "He's wasting a lot of gas around the ridge, trying to find a path down here." She looked out into the valley hidden in a cloak of white. "For the first time, I'm glad those machines make so much noise. We'll hear when he gets close."

It was a good point, but if the man retreated, that would only give them a temporary reprieve. This guy wouldn't give up so easily, not after he'd pursued her like this. Which meant she wasn't safe in her cabin. It was something else he needed to figure out, but for now, they needed to get going before it got dark.

David called Maple onto the sled, but she just looked up at Rain.

"It's okay, girl," said Rain. "Go on. I'm coming, too."

The dog bounded through the deep snow and climbed onto the rescue sled. David took another piece of dried meat from his pocket.

"Can she eat beef jerky?" he asked over his shoulder. "A buddy of mine made it. I gave her a bit of it earlier."

Rain grinned. "Now I know how you got her to come with you."

"She did until…"

"Until what?"

Until the path broke off for the ridge. That was why Maple had tried to steer him the other way. The dog had been right. Rain had gone up that path, and then she…

No, he wasn't going to think about her jump. He wasn't going to consider all the ways that could have gone wrong.

"Never mind. Let's get going."

David started across the cookout ledge, following the paths he'd created on the way in. He hadn't been here in years, and he struggled to dam up the memories that leaked from the landscape, memories of the way it used to be so easy between Rain and him. This wasn't the time for nostalgia. A new dusting of snow had fallen, but the weight of the sled pushed it down, packing the trail. When he got to the path out of their old territory, he breathed a sigh of relief and turned around to check Rain's progress. Her boots were only sinking a foot or so. The tightness in his shoulders eased a little. The less strenuous her hike up this side of the mountain was, the more he'd be able to focus on what lay in front of them.

He skied out onto the mountainside, and a gust of wind smacked him across the face.

"It's going to be a tough climb," he said over his shoulder.

"Tough to keep ourselves pointed in the right direction, too," she called over the wind.

Flurries whipped around the mountainside, shrouding the granite peaks of Crystal Summit in white. The clouds had moved in, bringing the kind of storm that dropped feet of new snow, not inches.

"We'll figure it out," he said, though the reassurance was as much for him as it was for her. He'd gotten himself out of much tighter situations before. He thrived in these kinds of scenarios, yet everything about this one felt riskier. He didn't want to think about why seeing Rain in a precarious situation was putting him on edge. It shouldn't, not all these years after he'd moved on with his life.

Rain took off her little backpack, unzipped it and pulled out a neatly coiled rope. "We should tie ourselves together so we don't get separated. You may not hear me call over the wind."

She was right, and David was thankful she wasn't distracted by their first meeting in five years. He, on the other hand, had to get his head on straight.

He took the end of the rope and secured it around his waist, and she did the same. Then he started up the incline. He pushed the sled in front of him, his skis sliding through the snow, but with each push forward, the wind countered his efforts, holding him back. Each step was a fight against the blizzard and the steep mountainside, and he wasn't sure he was winning. If they could only get a little higher, the granite face would be in view, leading them to the summit pass. But that presented a different danger. If they missed the pass and traveled farther, they'd hit icy, wind-packed snow, then a steep drop. In such low visibility, that could be fatal.

David turned the sled farther up the hill, testing the limits of his strength. With each step, he slid back, so he sped up and pointed his tips out farther, feathering up the mountain. He pushed himself harder until he started to sweat. Temperature was a tricky balance outside in the winter. Hypothermia was the obvious risk, but too much heat would make his thermal layer wet with sweat, which could easily chill him as soon as he slowed down.

David glanced down at Maple, who was looking up at him from the sled, alert. She was a big dog, and her fur was thick, but he wondered how long she could weather this snow before she got chilled. His thoughts wandered to Rain. Was she warm enough? She knew more about outdoor survival in the mountains than he did, but would she tell him if she was struggling? Five years ago she would have, but today he wasn't sure.

A tug of the rope shook him out of his thoughts. David stopped and looked over his shoulder as Rain approached.

"The snowmobile," she said, her voice low. "It's close."

Between the wind and his heavy breaths, he hadn't noticed anything else. He stilled himself and listened. The low whine of the motor hummed. It was hard to tell whether the noise was coming from the ridge or the pass. Chances were good that the guy couldn't spot them through the blizzard, but if he was on the narrow summit pass, they'd run right into him. They'd have nowhere to go.

The motor idled somewhere just above them. David stood, waiting, all the questions that he'd pushed aside flooding in. He knew this wasn't the time for them. Years of training told him to handle the situation at present and ask questions later, but he couldn't hold himself back.

"Why is this guy chasing you?" he said, keeping his voice low.

Rain looked up at him, her brown eyes filled with pain. "My brother was into something bad. I don't know what it is, but now this guy wants it from me."

"Even after Brandon's death?" Too late, the thought occurred to David that just mentioning her brother's death might hurt.

"Yeah, that's what worries me."

David swallowed back the wave of fear that came with her words. "Whatever it is, he's not giving up. It seems to be worth a lot to this guy."

"I can handle it. I'm pretty sure he wants me alive." She looked less certain about that than she sounded.

He didn't answer. They could argue that point once they were out of the storm. A few more long minutes passed, and then the motor gunned. The sound faded, dampened behind the granite peaks. David started again, heading uphill. The visibility was low enough that the sled hit rock before he saw it. He breathed a sigh of relief. They were almost at the summit pass. The snow was even deeper here, banked against the rock. Eventually, they passed the last of the trees. They'd reached the pass. He rounded the granite wall with care and followed the rock face around, then down until they hit trees again. He waited for Rain to catch up. When she did, her breaths were coming fast.

"The snowmobile's motor shut off," she panted. "It means the guy is somewhere around Crystal Lake. Somewhere nearby."

The idea settled like lead in his gut.

"Let's get down to the road and talk." That would

give him a little time to figure this out. He gestured to the sled. "Maple would love some company, now that we're headed downhill."

Rain looked like she wanted to protest, so he added, "Just in case you're going to argue with me, consider that if you ride, you won't leave footprints on this side of the mountain."

"I wasn't going to argue. I just don't want..." She let out a sigh. "Never mind."

He could guess some of the things she didn't want right now, and he was feeling the same way. She also looked too tired to press her point, which made him uneasy. Rain untied the rope around her waist. He did the same and handed his end back to her, and she coiled it and stowed it into her backpack. Then she scooted Maple up on the sled and sat down.

Downhill was significantly easier, both because the exertion was less and because Rain was safely in view. He told himself he'd feel like that in any rescue situation. David steered the sled back and forth down the hill, and they zigzagged their way to the road that circled Crystal Lake. The forest was quieter, with the wind at his back and the snow muting the sounds as it fell, adding another layer to the forest floor. The mountain was deceptively peaceful, and Rain was here. His heart sped up as those two thoughts connected. It was a dangerous feeling, so he reminded himself of how easily she had walked away five years ago.

He brought the sled to a stop at the edge of the road. In front of them to the left, he could make out the outline of Rain's cabin, dark in the shadows of the forest. To the right, the lights from his family's place glowed through the falling snow.

Rain climbed off the sled as if she were getting ready to walk away. He ignored the way this echoed in the wounds of their past and focused on his immediate concern. "You didn't recognize the guy when you saw him?"

Only a handful of cabins dotted the land around the lake. When he was younger, his family used to know everyone, at least by sight. Maybe not anymore.

Rain shook her head. "But he greeted me as Brandon's sister."

And he knew where her cabin was.

"So he's either staying in one of the cabins across the lake or at the old campground."

Rain nodded, like she was thinking the same thing.

The campground was only open during the summers, but people wandered in at all times of the year. As long as they were quiet and didn't leave trash, residents left the visitors alone. David looked past Rain's cabin, into the veil of white. If the man was at the campground, he wasn't far from Rain's cabin. She shouldn't go back there alone.

"I think it's better if the lights stay out at your place, at least until we know where this guy is," he said.

She looked over her shoulder at him and raised her eyebrows, probably at the *we* in that sentence.

"You should stay at our cabin, just for the night." She started to shake her head, so he added, "It's the payment I'm asking for my rescue services."

Rain let out a dry little laugh. "That's not fair."

If it meant she was safe for the night, he didn't care if it was fair or not.

"If we go to your house, our tracks will lead there." She frowned and added, "What if he follows us?"

"I'm going that way, so those tracks are unavoidable. But right now, the tracks to your house aren't."

She was quiet, and David was sure she was trying to think of another reason to say no. Maybe they could start in the right direction before she came up with one.

"My sister is at our cabin, and she was making soup before I left," he said. "She'll be thrilled to meet Maple."

"And probably less thrilled to see me."

He didn't bother answering. They both knew that was true.

Chapter Three

Rain squatted in front of the heavy wooden door to the Hernandez family cabin, brushing ice chunks out of Maple's fur with her gloves. The dog wouldn't hold still, wagging her tail and turning each time Rain went for her back legs.

"Maple, sit," she said, smiling a little. "You can't drip all over their cabin."

She pulled off the last ice balls, then looked out into the twilight. The snow was falling hard, and the tracks they'd made had turned into soft indents. The snowmobile's engine was still quiet, so they were okay…for now. But she was a little preoccupied by the idea that she'd made her own danger David's. And now Isabel's. It was one more reason both of them would be wary of her.

Rain would have been crazy to refuse David's offer just because she didn't want to face their past, but that didn't make these moments any more comfortable. She smoothed the fur over Maple's ears once more. "I'm stalling. Better just to get this part over with, right?"

Maple wagged her tail in agreement.

"Here we go."

Rain braced herself as she stepped over the threshold of the cabin, trying to keep the flood of memories at bay, but the scent of the pine floorboards, mingled with that of the spicy tomatoes and chilies wafting from the kitchen, derailed her plans. Sopa Azteca. It was a Hernandez family tradition to make a big pot of it before a family gathering. David and Isabel must be up here getting the place ready for one of those gatherings…or maybe not. So much had changed in the last five years, and she couldn't pretend to know the way their family worked anymore.

Rain unzipped her coat, pulling it off first, then shed her boots and snow pants. She hung up the pants and coat in the closet racks, just like she used to, and propped her boots on the mat next to the door. She balanced her gloves and hat on top of the radiator, the way everyone in the family did. And in that moment, the past didn't feel so far away. But the feeling faded the instant that thought fully formed. Her own family was gone, and her relationship with David was long over. Too much had happened to ever go back.

There was a dark brown towel on one of the racks, and she used it to dry Maple. She smoothed it over her coat as she listened to the hum of conversation coming from the kitchen. David's low voice and Isabel's higher one let loose in Spanish. Rain didn't catch what they were saying, though Isabel didn't sound too happy. But that was to be expected. After all, Rain had broken her brother's heart.

Rain had taken special care to learn Spanish, far beyond the basics, when she and David started dating so she could be more a part of their family. She used it occasionally as a nurse, but her skill with the language was rusty. Maybe it was better that way. Rain wasn't sure she wanted to know what Isabel thought of the situation she'd just pulled David into.

She checked the hallway mirror, tracing the scratches from the fall down her cheek. Lucky, very lucky. Her short brown hair was a matted mess, and she ran her fingers through it a couple times before giving up. Rain took a deep breath and then walked out of the front hallway, onto the familiar red rug David's parents had brought back from Jalisco years ago. She glanced at the mantel, then looked away. It was still filled with family photos, but she was sure the one with David and her was gone. The family had had every reason to remove her off the mantel. David's tía Maribel had taken the photo just after they'd gotten engaged. Rain had buried her own copy of it in one of the boxes in the back of her closet, but she could picture it. They'd been standing out on the dock, with Crystal Lake shimmering in the background. She hadn't thought about it in five years, at least not on purpose.

The Hernandez cabin was large, with high ceilings and enough bedrooms for David, his parents, his sister, his aunt, plus any other relatives who dropped in. Growing up, Rain's family had always just been the four of them. There were occasional cross-country visits with the grandparents, but even if her relatives had lived closer, she wasn't sure they'd see them more than they did. When she was young, Rain had wished her own family were a little bigger, a little closer. But wishes didn't always come true.

She crossed the living room and stopped just outside the kitchen.

"She'll hurt you again," said Isabel.

"It's in the past," said David, then switched to English. "She's in a tough spot right now."

Rain cringed. It was painful to hear that sympathy in his voice. *Poor Rain.* It sounded too much like pity, and after all these months without any family, she was sensitive to it. Somehow, pity made her feel more alone. It was especially hard to hear it from David, who, after her parents' death, had helped her feel less alone in the world. She should have been glad to hear this distance from him, glad to hear he'd moved on. Leaving him, hurting him like that, had been hard. It was a maze of guilt and feelings she didn't want to enter again. She was sure he didn't, either.

Rain rounded the corner into the kitchen before the conversation continued.

"Hi, Isabel," she said. "Sorry about intruding."

Isabel shrugged and gave her a tight smile. "David explained what happened. I'm glad you're okay."

There was an awkward pause. Five years ago, Isabel would have crossed the room to hug her. Today her old friend just nodded at her, polite but distant. But Maple didn't know any better, so she wandered into the kitchen, stopping by David for a scratch behind the ears before saying hello to the new human. Isabel squatted and offered her hand, and Maple licked her.

"I hope it's all right that I brought a dog in here," said Rain.

Isabel kept her gaze on Maple. "You're welcome here."

Rain also didn't miss Isabel's warmer tone for the dog.

"Fifi will be up here in a few days, so we even have food for you," David added.

Fifi. Tía Maribel had gotten the fluffy little white mop of a dog years ago when David and Rain were in high school, and she, Brandon, Isabel and David had spent that first summer trying to teach the puppy tricks. Fifi loved people enough to try, day after day, even though nothing much stuck beyond "sit" and "shake."

"Stay" was hopeless. Fifi couldn't stand being left

alone while everyone else walked away. Now that she was older, Rain understood that dog a little better.

Rain wanted to ask about Fifi, about Tía Maribel and their parents, but the wary look in Isabel's eyes reminded her that this was far from a social call. Rain also knew it was her job to try to mend their relationship, not Isabel's, so she said, "Thank you for coming to Brandon's funeral."

Isabel and Mrs. Hernandez hadn't stayed for the reception, but Rain still appreciated their presence.

Isabel lifted her gaze, her expression softer. "I'm so sorry about what happened. We all miss him."

Something in Isabel's voice, a note of real sorrow, hit Rain unexpectedly, and she blinked back the tears that threatened to well. These moments still crept up on her sometimes. She didn't know how long it would be like this, and sometimes she suspected it would never go away. But she didn't want Isabel and David to see her this way.

"Thank you," she said when she was sure her voice wouldn't shake. "I miss him every day."

The kitchen was silent, a little less tense now. Rain felt a strange lightness of relief inside, as if, for just a few moments, she was sharing the weight of her loss. There had been moments at Brandon's funeral when it felt like God had lifted it, brought everyone together, but in the months afterward, the sorrow had settled on her, heavy and oppressive. People tried to help, but they didn't know him, and, in his last years, her brother had become quiet and secretive. It made grief so isolating, with just Maple and her to remember all the good parts of him.

But in the Hernandez family kitchen, so warm and familiar, that lift came again. Isabel's sympathy was for her brother as Rain wanted to remember him. Lively. Happier. David and Isabel knew many sides of Brandon, including the best sides of him. The sadness still sat in her chest, reminding Rain of its presence with every breath, but it was bearable, less suffocating. She took a deep breath, letting the lightness fill her.

"Thank you," she repeated.

"I'm going up to dig out some extra sheets and do a little more cleaning," said Isabel after a while. "Help yourself to the soup. I finished it while you were gone."

Isabel elbowed David in the ribs, and he put his hands up in the air. "Next time, you take the rescue sled, and I'll stay back to cook and clean."

"No next times, God willing," she said with a frown.

Except Rain's problems weren't over. The man with the gun had retreated, but he'd be back. And Isabel was making it clear she didn't want her brother to get involved. David met her gaze, his eyes serious, as if he were making the same calculations as she had.

"You need to call the police before the cell towers go out." He said it with the authority of a firefighter, someone used to making decisions in the face of danger.

Rain sighed and shook her head. "What would I say to them? 'A man threatened me with a gun, but I don't know who he is, where he is or what he wants. Plus, he was wearing ski goggles, so I can't identify him?' What can the police do with that information?"

"They'd check out your cabin, maybe knock on some doors." He sounded less certain now.

"And then they'd leave because there's nothing to go on," she finished. "That's assuming they're willing to brave the storm. We both know storms bring all sorts of emergencies, so chances are good they wouldn't come until after it blows over."

David frowned, and she was fairly sure he saw her point. Even if the police came across the man, they wouldn't know it. But it could make the guy more volatile.

"What's the alternative?"

That was where she was stuck. Her thoughts were jumbled after the fear and shock of the confrontation, mixed with...well, whatever she was feeling about seeing David again. "I need some time to think this through. The man said I have until noon tomorrow."

"Then we'll discuss a plan early in the morning, after we've rested," he said. "I'll get the meal set up, and you can set the table."

Rain tried to ignore the warmth his words brought her, especially the *we* part. She wasn't alone in this, at least for now. David grabbed an avocado from the fruit basket and cut it in half and then sliced it as she took the bowls down from the cabinets. His hand brushed against hers as he took them from her, so natural and intimate that it startled her. Rain looked away before he noticed the color rising to her cheeks.

When they were seated at the long dining table, Rain said her own silent grace. She didn't realize how hungry she was until the first taste of the rich, spicy chicken broth, cut with the creamy freshness of avocado. She let out an audible sigh and tried to focus on the taste rather than the memories the soup brought back. Rain had so many questions for David, but she wasn't sure where asking them would lead.

David broke the silence. "Are you still working in the ER?"

She shook her head. "I transferred to the eye clinic not long after…"

Rain let the sentence trail off. But David seemed to know what she had left unspoken.

"I'm sorry I didn't come to Brandon's funeral."

"I understand," she said. Some part of her had been hurt that he didn't come, but mostly she'd been relieved. It would have been hard not to lean on him for support.

"I was out on a wildfire assignment in Southern California," he said. "My sister didn't tell me until I came back."

Of course that was where he was.

"Are you still going out for the wildfire season?" she asked.

He nodded. Even after five years, hearing about the wildfire work scared her. It was a reminder that she had made the right choice. He must have seen that on her face.

"You were right about the way I live my life. I haven't shied away from risks." He paused, then added, "I just wish we could have talked it over instead of you deciding to leave without discussing it."

The memory of the day he'd been rushed to the hospital for smoke inhalation was a blur of panic, fear and pain. She didn't remember most of it, and she still didn't want to. To know that he'd willingly walked into a raging wildfire—and he would do it again if he lived—that was too much. She'd waited until he was discharged, and then, when he was safely at home, she'd brought back the ring. He had called her selfish, and in a way, she agreed with his assessment.

Because what she really wanted was for him to give up his career. It was one of the main reasons she'd never talked much about this issue with him. Rain knew it was selfish to the core for her to ask him to give up what he loved, give up saving people's lives, just so she could sleep better at night.

"I'm sorry," she whispered. "I know it wasn't fair, but that feeling in the hospital, after all I'd been through with my parents, and then with my brother and the debt—"

"What debt?"

Rain bit her lip. She'd only hinted at it back then, not wanting to weigh their relationship down with yet another downturn in her life. But the sudden loss of their parents had left her and Brandon with a trail of debts that followed her to this day. She still hadn't sorted through all of her brother's papers, so she wasn't sure of the state of her brother's financial situation, but she was barely making all her own payments.

"It's not important," she said. "But I was worried for him, worried for you... It was enough to shake my faith."

She paused, then forced herself to continue. "I told myself to trust that God wouldn't give me more than I could bear, but it felt like a lie. If I'd talked to you about how it felt to see you in the hospital, if I'd let one more emotion in, I would have broken."

Please understand. It was hard to think about this part of their past, but time had passed, and she was stronger now. She could handle it, at least for today. But nothing had really changed from that day she left. David still walked toward danger, not away from it, and even if that was a part of him that she admired, she never could bear another family loss again.

It was that fear that had kept her away from him.

There were so many times she'd been close to picking up the phone to hear his voice, to apologize for the way she'd left him so abruptly, but at the time, she couldn't handle anything else. Still, it was hard to face the sadness she knew she'd caused for him.

Just sitting next to David, the steam coming from his bowl, his dark eyes focused on her, reminded her of why it had been so hard to leave him. But her heart was still raw and tender from the last battering. It wouldn't survive another blow.

Silence fell again as she slipped into her own thoughts, but David pulled her out again.

"Two years ago, I lost my closest friend in one of the big fires," he said, looking past her, out the window into the darkness. "We'd promised we'd evacuate a community, and we were most of the way through that when the wind changed. The flames were coming quickly, and we were scrambling. Hakeem went back in to get the last group who needed help, but…none of them came out.

"He left behind a wife and baby. Their families came to help for a while, cooking meals and doing the laundry, but when they all left, Angela and the baby were alone. So everyone at the station took turns helping." David turned to look at her. "Sometimes, when I was there, I found myself wondering why God had allowed this to happen to Hakeem and his family."

Rain had the urge to reach for his hand but stopped

herself. That wasn't her place anymore. She was just here to listen.

"But I also thought, this was why you left," he continued. "Because something like this could happen. I guess I'm just saying that even though it hurt when you broke off our engagement, I think I understand why you did it. I think you made the right choice."

The next morning, David stood in the kitchen, scrambling eggs while Isabel cut up tomatoes and avocadoes. For most of the night, David had lain half awake, listening for the sound of the snowmobile. But the night had been quiet, the snow blowing against the window panes. Rain and Maple had disappeared into one of the guest bedrooms shortly after dinner, and he hadn't heard a sound from that direction since. At least one of them had gotten some rest.

Seeing Rain again had shaken him a little yesterday. Time had healed some of the rawness, and the stab of pain and loneliness had eased. The good feelings that threatened to return, the warmth, the affection, the feeling that he could sit next to her and listen to what she said—those were tinged with wariness. Her eyes were so full of sadness and regret, and that old ache, that drive to comfort her, to protect her from the harshness of life, was back. And with it came the anguish, the feeling that a piece of his life, a piece of him, was missing. It warred with a different kind of hurt, one tinged with mistrust. After he'd come home from the hospital, he'd needed to lean on her a little. Instead, she'd left. He'd lashed out, calling her selfish. He regretted speaking those words, but he hadn't forgotten the betrayal he'd felt that day.

And he had to put it aside for today because there was no way he was going to allow her to go back to that cabin alone.

"You're awfully quiet this morning," said Isabel.

"A lot to think about," David said. "You know I'd do this for anyone."

"I know you would. Even someone who may hurt you again." She sighed. "You put yourself aside for others, and I love that about you. It's just… Be careful. We know how this can go."

He'd been thinking about this all night long. "Just try to be understanding this morning."

Isabel gave him a soft smile. "I'll try. For you."

His sister disappeared upstairs and returned shortly after with Rain and Maple. Rain was freshly showered and dressed in one of Isabel's sweatshirts and leggings, so David figured that was a step in the right direction. She was quiet, and he was fairly sure this meant she had come up with a plan, one that likely didn't include him. He was ready for this possibility. As she sat down at the table, the crack of a gun shattered the warmth of the cabin. Rain turned to him, her eyes wide.

"Do you have cell service?"

He shook his head.

"I don't, either."

The window for calling for help had closed, and if past storms were any indication, service wouldn't be up until the storm was over.

The momentary fear in her eyes was turning to focus. "That wasn't far away. And it's not even close to hunting season."

Who would shoot a gun in this weather? David was coming to one ominous conclusion, and he didn't like it.

"I need to figure out what the guy is after," Rain said. "He's been watching me, and he's going to come after me until he gets what he wants, so I have to determine what that is."

David tried to ignore the twist in his gut as Rain so casually discussed being hunted by someone.

"The man has a gun." He was trying to keep his voice even, but frustration was leaking in.

Isabel frowned. "Why don't you just wait out the storm in our cabin? Once the road is plowed, you can... I don't know..."

That was the problem. Rain didn't know what to do besides run away, but how did she run away from someone she couldn't even identify?

"I have to figure out something about who he is, what he wants...something I can take to the police," she said. "You heard the gunshot. He puts everyone up here on Crystal Lake in danger. I can't just sit back if he's out there, searching for me. What if he starts knocking on cabin doors?"

"In a storm?" David swiped a hand over his face, trying to hold back his frustration. How could she discuss this so calmly?

"I know my way around here in the storm, and he doesn't. Besides, I'm not going after him, just trying to figure out what's going on so I can protect myself."

David listened carefully, picking up on all the still-familiar signs. She wasn't speaking particularly forcefully, but the resolve in her eyes had hardened. She was going to do this, no matter what he said. There was a recklessness about this determination to go at it alone that scared him. Did she feel like she had nothing to lose? The idea brought on a wave of unsettling emotions that he had to switch off. Frustration threatened again, tinged with exasperation. There was only one way to deal with this.

"You're better off with someone else along. I'll come with you," he said. At least he could make sure she didn't do anything rash. Before she could protest, he turned to Isabel. "Can Maple stay with you here in the cabin? She's probably safer that way."

"Of course," said Isabel, but her frown suggested she wasn't happy with his decision to follow Rain into the impending storm.

Rain's gaze flickered over to David. Now she had to choose between having him along and taking Maple.

She tilted her head to the side. "You really want to be a part of this?"

"I already am. Besides, I'd also feel better having Maple here with Isabel."

The rev of a snowmobile's engine broke into the warmth of the cabin. Rain met David's gaze. Was the guy out searching for her?

"How's your ankle?"

Rain shrugged. "Better."

He heard what she didn't say: it wasn't fully healed.

"Right now, I know nothing, and that leaves me vulnerable," she said. "I need to know where this guy is and what he's after."

Isabel raised her eyebrows. "You want to take our snowmobile?"

"We're probably better off without it," said Rain. "Easier to stay under the radar." She studied Isabel like she was thinking through scenarios. "Besides, you and Maple need it, just in case."

"Are we going on skis?"

Rain nodded. "If I can borrow a pair."

"But you still have a snowmobile in your garage?" asked David. They needed an escape plan.

"Yes, but it'll take some work to get it gassed up and ready." Rain tilted her head to the side a little. "We used to butt heads a lot."

David let out a little laugh. "You could say that."

Most of the time, that wasn't a bad thing. Both of

them liked to be in charge, and they'd come up with all sorts of ways to decide who would lead. He'd always liked this about their relationship...that is, until the end, when she'd taken the lead and left him.

"If you're coming with me, I want the final say in what we're doing," she said. "This is my problem to deal with."

"Okay." In principle, he could agree with this, but dozens of scenarios could prove opposite. David was also aware that she'd try to block him from coming with her if he voiced those concerns, so he figured it was better to take that argument up later, when he needed it. "What's the plan?"

"First, look through my cabin to see if Brandon left something behind, and then figure out who and where the guy with the gun is. We'll start with the campground, then work our way around to the cabins on the other side of the lake."

The campground made the most sense for someone who wanted to keep under the radar. Easier to come in and out without a trace.

"I'll look for a license plate or some way to identify him." Rain glanced at him. His displeasure must have shown through, because she added, "I'm not planning to get close, of course."

He blew out a breath. How often did things go as planned? But David held back his instinct to warn her and went along with her idea. "We'll pack up, and when this guy goes in to refuel, we head out."

And head toward danger, not away from it. He'd done this his whole life, but somehow, knowing Rain would be walking toward danger with him changed everything.

Chapter Four

The fastest way to Rain's place from David's cabin was across the frozen lake, but that route was out of the question. Far too exposed, even in the blowing snow. She'd also ruled out the road because of the tracks they'd make leading back to Isabel and Maple. Last night's tracks had been buried in the new snow. Today they weren't taking that chance again. The best way to stay invisible was to head through the forest. It was also the hardest route.

Rain skied through the untouched snow, over the uneven ground of covered rocks and fallen branches far beneath them. The trees above sagged under the heavy white pillows piled on top. A few snapped under the load, but most bent lower and lower until the snow slid off in a mini-avalanche, onto the ground below. It was eerily quiet in the forest, just the gusts of wind that blew thick flakes everywhere in their path. Her white jacket and black snow pants had dried overnight, but she'd ditched her own orange hat for a white loaner from Isabel. Isabel's ski boots were a little big, even with two layers of socks, but they were stiff enough to support her ankle. So far, her ankle wasn't bothering her too much.

David followed behind, the swish of his snow pants a comfort in the quiet forest. She wasn't on her own. Whatever she had to face, he was there to back her up, at least for now. When she dialed his number, maybe there was some part of her that had understood he wouldn't leave anyone to face dangers alone. She also couldn't forget that, in the end, this was why she'd left him.

But they were working together, so she focused on the questions that had been plaguing her all night. Yesterday, she hadn't thought further than getting to safety, but as she forged through the winter landscape, her mind wandered to what the man on the snowmobile wanted. Something illegal to bring over the California border. As far as she knew, that could be anything from fruits to rare animals to weapons... Rain's gut twisted at that thought. *Please don't let it be weapons.*

But everything about the man's pursuit rattled ominously inside her. She couldn't shake the feeling that this afternoon could easily turn into more than just a quick reconnaissance trip. Where was the man on the snowmobile? And what would she find in her brother's room?

Before they left, she'd focused her energy on packing whatever lightweight things she could find that might give them an advantage. They'd replenished their food and warm drinks, and she searched the Hernandezes' house for things that they might need if their day went off the rails. Rain's reflective blanket and extra water bottle were in her backpack. She'd hunted around and found a basic first aid kit in their hall closet, with the usual contents like bandages, alcohol wipes, gauze and tweezers. She threw it all into a plastic bag, along with a Swiss army knife, a pencil and paper, a bandanna big enough to serve as a sling, and a roll of duct tape. The last item had earned her a side-eye from David.

"What exactly are you preparing for?" he'd asked with a little laugh.

She'd shrugged. "Eventualities."

After a few years as a nurse in the emergency room, she'd seen enough to learn that being prepared was everything, even if it meant thinking about worst-case scenarios. Rain had given Maple an extra hug before she left, too, trying not to think of said worse-case scenarios.

They made their way through the forest, tracing a path around the lake until they reached a clearing. She paused, peering through the veil of snow at the familiar landscape. Her cabin stood, dark and still in the storm, the roof of the place piled high in white. The house was built on a hill that sloped down toward Crystal Lake. From the front, only one story of the cabin was visible; there was a bottom floor that was accessible only from the back. She searched the hill and the backyard for snowmobile tracks, but she could see nothing from this side of the cabin. The place looked empty, lonely, or maybe this feeling was just the loneliness that had dogged her since she'd arrived. Back in Auburn, friends, her job and her church had filled her life. But here, looking at the empty cabin, the place where Brandon's life and hers came together, she felt a stark reminder of her losses.

"See anything?" The low rumble of David's voice came from next to her.

"Not from this side."

"Same," he said. "You ready to check it out?"

Rain bit her lip. She *should* be ready. This was why she'd come up to Crystal Lake in the first place: to step back into the cabin, into the life she used to share with her family. But it wasn't just the loss she'd be facing. She needed to search for evidence that her brother had been involved in something bad, something that linked him to the man who was threatening her. Was she ready to face whatever she might find out about Brandon? She swallowed.

"Can we, um—" she glanced at David "—can we check out the campground first? Then I'll be ready."

He looked at her, his eyes full of questions, but he didn't ask them. Instead he nodded, then started forward. They skied across her property, her cabin on one side, the flat, frozen lake on the other, glittering in the afternoon sun. Then they were back in the forest, weaving around pines and firs. The hum of a generator greeted them long before they arrived at the park. They wove between trees and over buried picnic tables until they reached the enormous piles of snow that the plow had left from earlier storms. The piles formed a sloping wall around the parking lot, hiding it from view. This area got some of the highest snowfalls in the country, and it took all sorts of equipment to keep the roads clear. There was probably a good fifteen feet piled up from previous storms.

Rain circled behind the hills, heading toward the sound of the generator. The park was heavily wooded, with tall pines and firs thick enough to block the view of the lake. The parking lot curved through the forest, and the last stretch had a view of Crystal Lake. If these people were there for the scenery, they could have chosen a beachside spot, but the sound was coming from much farther back, tucked away into the forest.

She stopped at the bottom of a large hill of plowed snow and turned to David. "It sounds like someone's parked right on the other side of this bank."

He nodded. "Let's dig ourselves a lookout at the top."

Rain took off her skis and stuck them into the snow, tips pointing at the sky. This snow was packed harder, so her boot got a better hold. Good, in case they needed to make a quick exit.

David took off his pack, dug out two plastic wedges and handed one to her. His lips curved into a small smile. "Just like old times."

She felt the corners of her mouth tug up. She remembered preparing, as a teenager, for an epic snowball fight. They would spend all afternoon building forts and making snowballs, she and David against Brandon and Isabel.

"Just like old times," she echoed.

But that spark of happiness died quickly. Brandon was gone, and David and Isabel weren't a part of her life anymore. *Your choice, Rain.* As David had confirmed last night, she had made the right choice. His friend who disappeared in the fire could have been him. The wife could have been her. It was dangerous to get lured in by the past, a past that neither of them wanted to return to.

When her parents died, her fears of being left alone hadn't set in right away. At first she clung to David, to Brandon, to Isabel, life rafts in an infinite sea of sorrow. But she'd picked herself up, slowly recreating some semblance of life without them. She could do it that time, but one thing was clear. She never wanted to be back there, stranded in that sea. With David, she couldn't help but give him everything, all of her. She didn't know any other way with him. And that meant risking losing everything again.

So she pushed aside her memories and started digging. The night had been cold, so the new layer of snow was still relatively light, but by the time they'd carved out a little ledge to hide behind, her arms were burning. She settled in, her back against the high wall. Now they could peek over quickly, a quieter and less clumsy option instead of crawling up and down.

David settled next to her. He fit their shovels into his backpack and pulled out a bag of trail mix. He pointed it in her direction, and she took off her glove and grabbed a handful.

"We still make a good team," said David, gesturing between them.

She tried to ignore the way the statement warmed her inside. "Too bad the other side is armed with more than snowballs."

Rain unscrewed the lid of her thermos and took a long gulp of hot chocolate, then stowed it back in her pack.

"Ready?" she asked.

He nodded.

She turned around and knelt on the ledge. David knelt next to her, and they rose until they could see over the top of the mound. The parking lot was mostly empty. There were a few trailers buried at the far end, down by the lake. Only one was nearby. About twenty yards farther down the wall of snow from them, a big, black truck was parked facing them, with a small camper hooked up to the back. The bed of the truck had a row of gasoline tanks stashed next to a hoist of some kind. A few feet away from the vehicles was a snowmobile. Her heart jumped. Was that the one she'd seen, with a black and silver nose? It looked right, but she wasn't sure. She gave herself a mental kick for not paying more attention to those details back on the ledge. Both the truck and the trailer were in good condition, and judging from the layer of snow around it, they had arrived relatively recently, not long before the storm started. About the same time as she had.

The thought rattled her nerves. Had the guy followed her in? Had he been watching her, not just here but back in Auburn, waiting for her to come to her cabin? Rain shuddered. Their exchange yesterday suggested it, and the eeriness of it was sinking in.

But this wasn't the time for these thoughts. She needed to focus on what they were doing right now.

"That may be the snowmobile I saw," she whispered to David.

"You're not sure?"

Her memories of the scene were clouded in fear, but she forced herself to search them. She shook her head. "We should write down the license plate, just in case."

But she didn't move to get the pen from her pack.

"You okay?" asked David, his voice barely there.

"Of course." She swallowed back her fear and nodded. "I just need a minute to think."

The truck and the camper were parked parallel to the snowbank, and she and David were positioned a little higher than the roof of the camper. Defensively, they were in a good position since the snowbank was too steep for a snowmobile. If anyone wanted to get to them, they'd have to pursue on foot, in thigh-high snow.

David took out a pen and jotted down the license plate, then pulled his binoculars from his pack and peered down toward the camper. Could he see inside the front windows?

"Notice anything?" she asked.

"No movement."

At least two feet of snow had fallen so far, burying the truck and camper. She eyed the snowmobile again. The snow was as high as the camper door, and a little path had been cleared from the door to the snowmobile and the truck.

"Water in the gas tank would put that thing out of commission," said David, glancing at her. "Just saying…"

"But that would mean one of us has to go down there."

"I could come back tonight."

"No." The word came with enough force to make her cheeks heat. "Too risky."

David opened his mouth to reply, but before anything came out, the generator on the back of the camper switched off. Silence rang in her ears. Only the sound of the wind remained, along with…a baby crying?

"Are you hearing that, too?" whispered David.

"Unfortunately, yes."

"Is that coming from this camper or one farther down?" His voice cut off as he peered into his binoculars. "Wait. I think I just saw a woman, holding the baby."

He passed her the binoculars, and she focused on one window, then another. For a moment, she caught a glimpse of movement, but she couldn't make out anything identifiable.

Rain passed the binoculars back and shivered. She was cooling down from sitting here, the wind whipping at their backs. "What kind of family event is this?"

David pulled back and reached for his pack, stowing the binoculars in their case.

"Either we're at the wrong place, or a baby is involved..." Her imagination took off as she pictured a woman, stuck with a man pursuing something nefarious. Or maybe she was in on it with the man. Either way, a baby changed the limits of what she was willing to do. "I think this rules out putting water in the gas tank, just in case."

David sat on the ledge next to her. "Good point."

It would be days before Crystal Lake was plowed out. She couldn't stomach even the possibility of stranding a baby here, no matter who their parents were.

David was watching her, his eyes intense, like he

was considering what she said. Snowflakes fell between them, covering his black hat and sticking on his dark eyelashes before they fluttered down. He sighed. "You're right. We'll just have to plan around it."

The squeak from the camper door startled her, and her attention darted to it. A man in a black coat appeared in the doorway. Rain stared at him, frozen, as her heart took off. Yes, that was same blue insignia on the breast she'd seen yesterday. This had to be the same guy.

David tugged hard on her coat, pulling her down. Rain's brain clicked back into gear as she scrambled out of sight. The squeak of the trailer door stopped, and her heart thumped harder.

"You're letting in the cold." A woman's voice came, muffled from behind the snowbank. "What's going on?"

"Thought I saw something," said the man.

Then the door slammed shut. Did he return to the camper, or was he coming this way? She turned to David, frantic, but he laid his hand on her arm, silently telling her to wait. She listened for clues about where the man was, but all she heard was the wind. Time stretched out, each thump of her heart a drumbeat that called out danger. Then there was a sound, a scrape of plastic on metal? Her mind ran through possibilities as more sounds came. David's hand stayed on her arm, his jaw tense. Then there was a whirr of a motor starting, and the sound of the generator rang over the snowbank.

"The generator," she whispered, relief flooding through her. "He came out to refuel."

David nodded, but he didn't look nearly as relieved. "He hasn't gone back in yet."

David did his best to put aside all the emotions that flooded him as he sat on the ledge they'd dug out, waiting for that guy to make his next move. Now wasn't the right time to process the protective instinct that had hit him with full force the moment he knew Rain was in danger again. It was an echo of who they used to be to each other, not who they were today. Instead, he thought about the extra-large black truck and the expensive-looking trailer with the baby crying inside. The more he thought about that, the more uneasy it made him. Whoever these people were, they wanted what Brandon had badly enough to get snowed into a remote mountain parking lot with a baby.

David couldn't hear anything other than the wind and the generator. The door to the camper still hadn't opened. If the man came toward them, would they hear him in time to escape? He glanced at Rain huddled next to him, still and alert. He wasn't taking any chances.

"We need to get out of here," he said.

Rain must have been thinking the same thing because she gave a little nod and started forward, sliding on her backpack as she eased herself down the embankment. David was right behind her, scrambling to fit his shoes into the ski bindings from a crouched position. He succeeded before Rain did.

"Go," she whispered. When he didn't move, she glared at him. "I'm right behind you."

He bit back another wave of protective instinct and started toward the nearest clump of pine trees. He pushed forward through the new snow, getting some distance before he glanced over his shoulder. What he saw made his heart stop. Rain was on her feet, right behind him, just as she'd said. But behind her, he could see the top of the man's head emerging over the snowbank. And all David could think about was that he shouldn't have agreed to go before her. Now she was the most vulnerable.

"Faster," he said in a low voice. "Don't look back."

She tucked her head as he turned around and took off, trying to focus on the trees in front of him, trying to trust that she could get out of this situation, too. But trust wasn't something that would ever come easily for him when it came to Rain.

"Looking for me?" The man's voice came from behind him. "Do you have my property?"

David sprinted forward, forcing himself not to turn around. He prayed Rain did the same. As he reached the tips of the first pine they were aiming for, the man's voice came again.

"And you brought company?"

David gave two more hard pushes and hid behind a tree, then another before coming to a stop. Rain came up close behind him. She ducked down, peering through the branches, her breaths coming fast.

"I can't tell if he has a gun, but he's definitely on foot," she panted.

"You have a few more hours to get me my shipment," the man called, his voice low and menacing.

David tried to get a better view of him, but all he saw through the tree were fragments of a red shirt under the black jacket. Was the guy coming toward them?

"We need to leave," he said. "If we head straight back from here, the trees will protect us."

It wasn't much, but it was better than nothing.

Rain took a deep breath, then exhaled. "You first."

David shook his head. Not a chance. "I'll be the tail this time."

She opened her mouth like she was about to disagree but decided against it. Instead, she took one more look through the trees and then started forward, in a direct line away from where the man was standing. The wind was picking up, drowning out the sound of the generator as they made their way through the forest. David looked back a few times, but the man wasn't following them. They'd caught him off guard, but he'd be ready next time. Would he wait until noon, or did they just shorten the dead-line? The idea sent a chill through David.

Rain skied in front of him, navigating around the covered landscape. The farther they traveled from the campground, away from danger, the more David's mind began to wander. The last time they'd skied together like this was the December before she left him. The holidays had been tough on her, the loss of her parents weighing a little heavier, but out in the forest, with the snow falling everywhere, all the heaviness seemed to fall away. It had been *Nochebuena*, Christmas Eve, and they'd skied halfway around the frozen lake, then headed back straight across it, the snow thick under them and the mountains rising up all around. He made some stupid joke, and she'd pushed him over and laughed with so much lightness. Then she'd come up next to him and kissed him. It was hard to believe how much things had changed since then.

Rain's cabin came in sight, peeking through the trees and the blowing snow. She stopped, waiting for him to catch up. David stared at the dark, still cabin. He had a bad feeling about going in there, especially since the man had just caught them watching him. He had to tamp down the strong urge to take control of the situation and call off the search.

"We shouldn't have gone to the campground first," she said quietly. "But I wasn't ready..."

David felt a tug in his gut as the sadness in Rain's voice hit him.

"We can talk about that later," he said gruffly. "Let's focus on what we're doing now."

She nodded. "We can check the front for footprints from the road to see if the guy has been here, then go in the back."

If it were up to him, he'd have her stay hidden, act as a lookout. He'd go in first, to make sure it was safe. But she was making the final calls today, so he nodded.

The snow was piled high, close to the first-story windows. Rain stopped at the corner of the house, and he came up next to her. In the front yard, he could make out long, flat prints, where it looked like the snowmobile had driven. The garage was close to the street for plowing convenience, but the tracks went up to the front door. A chill wound down David's spine. He had been right to insist that she stayed at their cabin last night. Otherwise, she would've been caught alone with this guy at some point.

"It looks like someone came and went," she said. "The tracks are relatively fresh. Do you think someone else is in on this, someone who's still here?"

"We can't rule it out."

She nodded.

The uneasiness was rising inside him, and with it, the urge to take over grew stronger. Finally, he broke down.

"What do you think about staying back, and I'll go in first?" he asked. "They're not looking for me."

Rain gave a sharp shake of her head. "They want me alive. Who knows what would happen if you surprised them." She hesitated, then added, "I can't let you take risks for me. Especially not after…"

She didn't finish that sentence, but she didn't have to. He knew what she was saying. *After I left you.*

David ignored the tightening in his chest. "It's my job to take these risks. I take this kind of risk every day. And facing a stranger with a gun isn't the worst I've seen."

There it was, the thing that had hung heavy between them until it had broken them apart. The risks he took every day on the job. But it was no use tiptoeing around the topic. She might have left him because of it, but today's plan wasn't about their old relationship. This was about their safety.

David wanted to remind her of the years of deescalation training he'd had. He wanted to tell her about all the tight situations his team had gotten themselves out of. He'd seen a lot as a firefighter, and he'd been sent in to rescue people who were more worried about getting arrested than getting out. He knew how to talk people down but also when to give up on that tactic. He regularly put his own life on the line, depending not only on his physical strength but on his negotiation skills. He'd carried people from all walks of life out of buildings because he believed he did not have the right to decide who lived and who died. It was why he didn't, and never would, carry a gun. Because a gun could so easily kill, and he never wanted to have that on his conscience. Instead, he dedicated himself to heading off conflict, and it had kept him alive so far.

Rain was quiet, and for a moment he thought she might be considering his proposal to go in first. But then she shook her head. "I know it's your job, but I'm the one who needs to search the cabin, to see if Brandon left anything behind, and we're running out of time. We don't know how soon the guy will be back."

Resigned, David let out a breath and nodded.

He stepped aside on his skis and turned around, then pushed off, gliding down the hill, to the ground-floor entrance, and Rain followed close behind. The snow covered half of the bottom-floor windows, but the porch roof outside the sliding door created a little area, clear from snow, to enter. Rain took off her skis and inspected the area around the entrance, probably looking for tracks or some kind of evidence of entry.

David stepped out of his skis and stuck them into the snow, next to Rain's. He left his poles next to hers and headed into the little cave-like entry. He dusted off his jacket and hat, and Rain shook off the snow, then fished into her pack and pulled out her keys.

The hallway was cool and dark, with empty coat hangers and shoe racks, but Rain didn't bother to take off any of her winter layers. They walked into the main room and past a sofa, their footsteps silent on the carpet. She led the way across the room, to the staircase. He should have kept his gaze trained forward, but the room was filled with their past. The sofa was an unremarkable brown, yet it was the place they'd watched movies, played cards, laughed, fought and made up, even long before their first kiss. He wondered if Rain ever thought about those days.

The door at the top of the steps was closed, and with every step, the stairway got darker, only a thin band of light escaping from under the door. If someone else was in the house, they weren't moving around. They were sitting, waiting. Only the swish of David's and Rain's winter gear disturbed the silence. The closer David got to the top, the harder his heartbeat pounded. The stakes were too high with Rain here, too high to block her out. He couldn't let her walk out the door, unprotected. David stopped at the top of the stairs and turned around. Rain looked up at him, her brown eyes large, and he felt a burst of warmth too strong to ignore. No, he really couldn't let her enter until he knew what the situation was.

"I need you to stay here until I call for you." He was trying not to sound like he was giving orders, but his voice was heavy and final. "Please."

She looked in his eyes and he felt like she could see right into him, like she could see his most vulnerable parts. It was painful to be vulnerable for her, after all they'd been through. She had seen all of him, and even then, she'd decided to leave him. He could never fully trust her again, not after she'd walked away from him without even talking to him first. And yet, a mixture of worry and hope was swirling inside him, and David had no idea how to handle it.

"You go first," she said. "But you better not get hurt."

Chapter Five

The basement door opened, and David slipped through it, out into the gray daylight. He closed the door behind her, leaving her in the darkness. Rain stood still, listening for clues, but her heart was thumping too hard to hear the nuances of the sounds. David's footsteps were quiet, and she strained to hear any shifts or creaks coming from the rest of the house. Was that the snowmobile engine in the distance? Or maybe it was her own fears getting the better of her. Because right now, as she waited alone, all she could think about was that day five years ago, sitting outside the emergency room, waiting for news. The only information she'd had was that the smoke inhalation had been bad enough that he might not make it.

That's in the past. He knows what he's doing.

She let these words run through her mind a few more times, but they did nothing to quell the fears.

Why was this so hard, despite all the years they'd been apart? He was no longer in her life, and while she would fear for anyone in danger, this felt worse. So much worse.

He took risks like this all the time, but the thought made the fear twist harder in her gut. She had let go of him, left him to avoid this feeling, yet here she was, slipping right back into it so easily. When she called him from the cookout ledge, she hadn't imagined these feelings would hit her this hard. It was as if she was wearing her insides on the outside once again.

It shouldn't feel like that. All she could think to do was bargain.

Please, Lord. Protect him.

David's footsteps stopped, and his voice rang throughout the house. "Search and rescue. I'm unarmed. Does anyone here need help?"

Rain couldn't help admiring his approach. Search and rescue came to help, not corner someone. If anything would help him stay safe, this would.

David's voice went unanswered in the silent house. There was a creak of a door, then another and another. Rain held her breath, waiting. It was the waiting that was pushing the limits of her fear, pushing the limits of her self-control. One moment, one wrong step, one twist of fate and everything could be over. She, of anyone, knew that was true. And with that understanding came the drive to open the door, not to just sit back and let events happen. That instinct warred with the knowledge that David really did know how to handle a situation like this better than she did. So she closed her eyes and put every ounce of her energy into praying.

"All clear."

David's words on the other side of the door were a flood of water over the fire of her fears, and she let the relief pour in for one long breath.

"Rain?"

"I'm here."

"Come take a look at this."

There was warning in his voice, so she took a steadying breath and turned the knob.

It took a moment for her eyes to adjust. The storm cast an eerie darkness over her cabin, and she looked around to see which direction David had gone. She spotted it immediately. Next to the bags she'd dumped onto the floor by the front door yesterday was a trail of puddles that led down the hallway, as if someone had walked through the house with snow on their boots and not bothered to clean it up. It was too much to be David's alone. Someone else had been here, inside her private space. She ignored the uneasiness that thought brought and followed the trail toward Brandon's bedroom.

Rain put a hand on the wall to steady herself. Just the idea of coming up to the cabin had been too much to bear since Brandon's death last year. She'd told herself that she'd be ready to enter it after she'd said goodbye, but she could barely stand under the weight of her loss. She'd never really be ready to face it.

Still, Rain straightened and forced herself to continue, through the shadows of the hallway, until she came to the door. David stood in front of her, blocking her view, and she prepared herself for the very worst. Everything inside her told her to run away, but David would help her through this. This thought alone kept her in place. Tentatively, she took a step, coming out from behind David's broad back, and looked in Brandon's room.

The first feeling that hit her was relief. No one else was here. It was only then she let herself acknowledge that she had been preparing herself to find someone taken hostage...or worse. But it wasn't anything like that. The room was a mess. The furniture had been moved away from the walls, as if someone had looked behind each piece, searching for something. The dresser drawers were half-open, with shirts and socks and long underwear hanging half out of them and spilled in piles on the floor. Papers and office supplies were scattered on the desk, as if someone had dumped the contents of the drawers on top of it. Brandon wasn't messy by any standards, and this was beyond disordered. Someone had searched his room extremely thoroughly.

She glanced up at David. "Someone's definitely been here."

"I wonder if they found what they were looking for," he said softly.

"If it was the guy from the campground, then my guess is no. He wouldn't be interested in me if he'd found a lead."

The surprise of finding Brandon's room in this state was doing a decent job of blunting her reaction, but the numbness wouldn't last. Rain took a last look around the room. "We should check the rest of the house."

David followed her down the hallway and stood close as she rested her hand on the doorknob to her bedroom. She took a deep breath, turned the knob and opened the door.

The scene was another punch in the gut, and fear tingled through her body. That man—surely that was who'd ransacked her house—had been in her room. He had gone through her things, overturned her life and rifled through it. The dam of emotions threatened to break, and she looked for something to hold her together.

She glanced up at David. He was studying her, his eyes hinting at something too close to caring. She was frozen to the ground, the dam swelling, leaking pain and loss and loneliness.

"Let's focus on what we came for," he said gently.

Rain swallowed and nodded, forcing out everything except David's voice.

"We'll assume that guy didn't find what he needed.

Is there any place Brandon would leave something just for you? Someplace other people wouldn't think to look?"

Had Brandon been aware of the danger he was in? Was he scared enough to leave some sort of clue for her to follow?

"I don't—" Rain stopped midsentence as an idea came to her. She walked out of her bedroom and continued down the hallway, to the living room. The pillows were pulled from the sofa, and some of the books spilled onto the floor, but not all of them. Thank God, not all of them.

Rain walked to the bookcase, stepping over a heap of books, and reached for *My Side of the Mountain*. She pulled it off the shelf, telling herself that this old hiding place was probably a dead end, trying not to hope. Not only would a clue help them figure out what the man was looking for. It would also be one more connection with the brother she had lost.

She looked up at David. "Remember how Brandon used to run away sometimes?"

David nodded. He probably hadn't forgotten how much it worried her, either.

She tapped the cover of the book. "This was how he told me where he was."

Her brother would get mad at her parents, and he'd disappear into the forest for days. He'd leave at night, usually after a big fight about something they wouldn't let him do. The first time had scared her so badly that when he came back two days later, she'd made him promise to leave her a note, just to tell her where he was going. He'd agreed, as long as she never shared it with anyone else. She hadn't. She even visited him sometimes, when she got lonely. Brandon was the one who discovered the system of caves on the other side of the summit, which was how they'd found the cookout ledge. As he'd gotten older, he ran away less often, and she'd forgotten just how much comfort the notes had brought. But when she was younger, she'd depended on them, enough that she'd burn them afterward, just to make sure her parents didn't find them. To make sure she never lost that connection. His notes were always in the same spot: in the back of *My Side of the Mountain*.

Rain stared at the cover, a mixture of excitement and wariness swirling inside her. She opened the book to the last page, and there it was, staring at her. An envelope. On the front of it, her name was printed in Brandon's cramped handwriting. She ran her fingers over the writing, and her heart gave a swoop of hope. Maybe Brandon was alive. Maybe he had written her to tell her where he was.

But emotions weren't logical, and at the moment, logic kicked in. Rain knew this hope was a fantasy. She had identified Brandon's body, and though he had been in a condition that she never wanted to see him, she had been sure of who it was.

"You all right, Rain?" David's voice was gentle, a

lifeline, reminding her that even if this surge of emotions threatened to pull her under, she wasn't alone.

"I haven't been in here since Brandon died. It was just…" Her voice wavered, but she forced herself to continue. "It was just too hard."

"Do you want me to look at it first?" There was so much compassion behind his words, and somehow, it made her feel even more vulnerable. She blinked back the tears that were welling, telling herself she had the rest of her life to mourn her brother. Right now she needed to focus on what Brandon had written in the letter.

If anyone had told her a year ago that her brother had left her a letter, she would've torn it open immediately. But as she looked down at Brandon's handwriting, she was no longer sure if she wanted to know what was in this missive.

Rain gave him a weak smile. "I have to look at it sooner or later, right?"

She opened the envelope carefully and pulled out the letter. She scanned it, the words jumping out at her, piercing her like knives, each little cut drawing more pain. But there was no escaping them. She took a steady breath and made herself read it aloud to David.

"Dear Rain,
    I'll be gone for a while, and I figure you'll be looking for me. I'm sorry I couldn't tell

you directly. I couldn't risk dragging you into this. But I promised never to disappear on you again, and I'm keeping my word to you.

I found a way out of debt, but it's gotten me into a tight spot, so I need to lay low for a while. Last year at a gun show, I met a guy who was looking for someone to take guns over the border from Nevada. He offered me enough to clear out of the debt from all the bills we racked up for rent, food and your college tuition, so I took the job."

Rain paused her reading as the heaviness sank in. Brandon's debts were partly her fault. He had insisted they had the money, and it wasn't until years later that she understood he'd taken out loans. She glanced up at David, wincing at his penetrative gaze. She'd never told him the extent of their money problems. Could David guess how much this mess was because of her?

He seemed to be able to read her line of thought, because he shook his head. "None of this is your fault, Rain. This was his choice, not yours."

Rain bit her lip. She wanted to believe that, but maybe she could have done something more...

"You don't have to read the whole letter now," he said quietly.

She shook her head and focused on the letter again.

"But when my payment came in after the

first shipment, it was a lot less than I was told. The guy said things changed with the delivery, but I think he just got greedy, so I held back the second half of the delivery until I got the money I was promised. I still have everything, hidden in one of the caves behind the cookout ledge, so stay away from there. If they find you, don't try to negotiate with these men— you can't trust them.

I'm sorry I had to leave you again like this. I know you're probably angry at me for disappearing, but please know that I did this to give us both a new chance. I hope it works.
Love,
Brandon."

Rain looked up at David. He was staring down at her, his expression grave.

"He's right. I *am* furious he did this." Her voice shook as she spoke, and it was only then that she realized she was crying.

David watched the tears spill over the rims of Rain's deep brown eyes, soaking her long, dark lashes. The urge to comfort her was unbearable. Growing up, she cried so rarely, and he tried not to think about how long she must have been holding it in. There were a dozen reasons to resist the urge, but he ignored them and gathered her in his arms.

Rain stilled for a moment, like she'd been caught off guard, and then, tentatively, she rested her cheek against his coat. After a soft sob, her arms came around his waist, and her body sagged against his. The weight of her sadness enveloped him, and he hoped she felt he was there. He wanted to lift the burden for just a little while. David told himself that he would have done this for anyone else, that this was his path in life, but he knew it was a lie. Everything with Rain had always been different, and for better or for worse, it still was. He had to wonder how this could be God's plan for him, knowing the pain it would bring when they parted ways again.

He moved one hand up her back to rest it in her hair, the way he used to do, but as his glove reached her neck, her body turned rigid. The rejection stung, but before his next breath, his insides froze. It wasn't his touch she'd reacted to. There was a buzzing noise from outside. The windows dulled the sound, and he'd been so caught up in Rain that he hadn't registered the whine of the snowmobile's motor in the distance. But it had been there for a while, and it was close. Very close.

David dropped his arms and took a step back, dread rippling through him. He'd gotten distracted and failed to pay attention to their safety. It was a rookie mistake, and he had made it. He had to get them out of this house.

"We need to go," he said, his voice hard.

Rain nodded, stuffing the letter into her jacket pocket. "You think we can make it out on my snowmobile? We need to pour in the gas and get it off its trailer."

"Maybe. If he doesn't come straight here."

Rain pulled on her gloves and started for the hallway, toward the door to the garage, just off the front entrance. But as they passed Brandon's room, the motor cut. The guy was here.

"Too late," he said. "We're stuck with skis."

They needed to get out of the house before the man got in. His mind worked through possible scenarios. Was the front door locked? The trail of water suggested the intruder had come and gone that route, which would mean it wasn't. Which indicated he would come too quickly for them to escape. If David stopped to lock it, they'd have a few more precious minutes. Lifesaving minutes. At worst, he'd face the guy alone, but there was a possibility he could talk himself out of it. Even in that scenario, Rain would have a good chance of getting away.

"Get on your skis and wait for me behind the trees," he said over his shoulder, his voice low. "Don't turn back. I'll be right behind you."

He passed the door to the basement and headed for the front hall. With each step, more risk calculations raced through his mind. In those brief seconds when the guy had stepped out of his trailer, David had studied the man's build. The guy was about the same height, but David was bigger. Working as a firefighter meant staying in top shape, whether it was from evacuating a building or hiking through the blazing heat of the California summer in full equipment to head off a fire. Instead of physical power, the man carried a gun, which brought its own advantages and disadvantages. The advantage was obvious— the ability to wound or kill from a distance. But that knowledge tended to come with overconfidence, a carelessness when it came to assessing danger. It also tended to make people reckless when cornered.

The fact that their assailant had a gun also meant he was willing to harm them. It was easy to forget this part of the equation, but this knowledge had been key in saving David's life more than once. Sadly, the world was built to give that willingness to harm others a short-term advantage. But despite all the ways his faith had been shaken over the last few years, David didn't believe God would let cruelty win.

His mind ran through each of these assessments as he raced through the hallway, coming up with possible scenarios and responses. Just a few more steps. But as David reached for the lock, the door came crashing into him.

He stopped the door with his boot, but not before the intruder took a step inside. Although the man was dressed in a black ski jacket and reflective goggles, David had no doubt who it was. The man froze in his steps.

"Who are you?" the guy demanded.

David didn't bother to answer, focusing instead on the problem at hand. If he pushed him hard enough... David shoved the door as hard as he could, throwing his full weight behind it. The door cracked and the guy stumbled back, but he managed to wedge his boot in the opening before David could shut it. David pressed his shoulder against the thick wood.

"I just want to talk to Rain." It sounded like the guy was gritting his teeth.

"Not a chance," he muttered.

David kicked at the guy's foot, but it was stuck there. He tried again.

"I have a gun," said the man.

"I know."

"I doubt that door will protect you."

David didn't want to find out. He heard a rustling, and he assumed the guy was going for his gun. Which meant his concentration wasn't on the door. David gently eased his weight off the door, then gave the guy's boot another swift kick. It worked. The man's boot moved back, and David shoved his weight against the wood again. The force pushed the boot the rest of the way out, and the door slammed shut with another crack. David clicked the dead bolt in place and spun around.

What he saw sent a shot of ice through his veins. Rain was standing right behind him.

Chapter Six

"What are you doing here?"

David's voice was low and furious, but his eyes blazed with something that looked more like fear than anger. His gaze was intense, the way she had imagined he looked as he ran into a fire. But right now, that gaze was directed at her. He had ordered her to leave, and she hadn't followed his orders. But he wasn't her superior, and it was her call to make, not his. What she'd witnessed was why she'd insisted on getting the last say on their plans. David was willing to walk into danger, and though he might be fine with that, she was not.

"Are you kidding? This is my problem to deal with," she murmured. "I wasn't going to leave you behind."

He glared at her. "This is a fine time to decide that."

It was an arrow shot straight at her heart, and it hit harder than she'd expected. She already had left him behind five years ago. Rain knew she deserved that reminder, but right now?

David swiped a hand over his face, like he was thinking the same thing.

"We don't have time to fi—" Before she could finish that word, a shot rang out, echoing through the cabin.

"Let's go," he growled, as she turned for the door to the basement steps. She ran down, taking two at a time, racing toward the hazy glow of daylight in front of her. Another shot sounded, and the man's voice came through the walls, muffled and menacing.

"He's still not on his snowmobile, so we have a few more minutes to get our skis."

There was another shot, and then the tinkle of glass shattering. Her window. The man was destroying her cabin. It was the only place she had left of her family, and he was invading it. *Material things can be repaired.* It was just living things that never came back.

Rain raced down the stairs and across the basement floor, towards the back door, as the intruder's footsteps thumped above her.

"I'm willing to give you the money you want," the man called.

But he could never give her what she wanted. Rain wanted her brother back, and the fact that this man didn't understand this shot a new bolt a fear through her. He thought that it was money that she would want out of this. This man either lacked empathy, or he was too preoccupied with his own worries to think strategically about her. Neither option boded well.

She entered the back hallway and fumbled with the door until it slid open. The man's voice came through the floor again. "You can make two hundred thousand dollars out of this. Think about how many problems go away with two hundred thousand."

He was right, she thought as she stepped out the door. That amount of money would cover the debts that she carried with her and maybe even get her ahead. Maybe she could even start saving for the impossible down payment that buying a house in California required. It would set her up for a life without the kinds of struggles that had dogged her and Brandon since the death of their parents.

But the money wasn't a temptation. Money made this way would never bring her peace. Knowing that she was helping to bring weapons into the state, weapons that were meant to kill people, would haunt her for the rest of her life. She gladly would trade that kind of guilt for a mountain of debt. Rain wondered if this guy could understand that.

As they stepped outside, the relief of cold air hit her in the face. They'd been inside too long, and she had started to sweat. Sweat was dangerous when she didn't know how long they were going to be out in the cold, but she could do nothing about it.

Rain looked around. The skis stuck out of the

snow like little flags, showing the man with the gun where they were the moment he looked out the window. It was a careless mistake.

"We should head for that group of spruces," she whispered to David above the wind, pointing into the forest. "It's downhill from here and gives good coverage. And then the skis work to our advantage. He'll have trouble driving through the denser clumps of trees on a snowmobile if he goes in there at all."

David muttered in assent, then added, "Don't look back for me if I'm behind you. Just go."

"That goes for you, too."

He frowned, and she wasn't sure if he was agreeing. "Let's go."

She grabbed her skis and laid them next to each other. She tried to step into the first binding, but nerves and the rush made her unstable, and she tipped to the side, her foot sinking deep into the snow. Rain pulled her boot out, her heart thumping. She looked up, and David was in front of her, ready to go.

"Go," she said. "He needs me, but he doesn't need you."

But he didn't move. Rain pulled her foot up and brushed the packed snow off the bottom, then slipped her foot into the binding. This time the boot slipped in and she clicked it shut.

A gunshot rang from above her, ear-splittingly sharp. It sent a shock wave through her body, and the ringing in her ears almost blocked out the cracks of glass shattering above her.

"Get out of here," David shouted.

Rain pushed off as hard as she could and glided down the slope. Behind her, more glass shattered as the guy shot at them through the window. David sped ahead of her, blazing a trail through the thick snow. The wind whipped at her face. Her heart pounded and her legs burned as she glided down the slope, toward the stand of trees.

She waited for another shot, but it didn't come. She entered the brush, the dark spruce branches scraping at her face, snow tipping everywhere, but she pushed forward. Between the branches, David was waiting for her. She came to a stop next to him, buried thick inside the curtain of green. He said nothing. Instead, he examined her face, his gloves gliding over her skin. He reached for her hat and pulled it off, shaking it into the snow. It took a minute to register what he was doing: checking for glass.

"Are you hit anywhere?" he asked, his voice gruff and curt.

"I…I don't think so." Everything was tingling and numb, and it was hard to register anything about her body right now.

"Take off your pack and shake it, just in case," he said. "We need to make sure. And then we need a plan."

Rain nodded, dazed. David was so good at his job.

She wouldn't have thought of any of this. Her mind was blank, and the gun shots were ringing in her ears. *Run*, her body seemed to scream. *Run*.

But Rain slipped off her pack and shook it toward the snow. Out of the corner of her eyes, she saw David doing the same. She found a piece of glass sticking out at the top of her pack, but otherwise, she had escaped unscathed. *Thank You, Lord*.

The snowmobile motor still hadn't turned on. It would any second now.

"If we go back to my cabin, there's a chance he'll follow us there," David said.

"I won't put Isabel in danger," she said flatly.

"Agreed. Our best odds are on the mountain. Then our tracks lead the guy away from the cabins, and we have the advantage of knowing the area. He'll have to go slow in this weather."

The snow was coming down harder, so visibility was low.

"You're right." Rain assessed the food status. They had packed light, enough for two days at the most. Drinks were limited, too. Snow would work for liquid in a pinch, though the cold was a risk. "If we can lose this guy, the caves by the cookout ledge are our best chance at shelter."

"*If* we lose him."

"There's a chance. We know this area, and he doesn't." She paused, trying to think through the situation. "I also think we should find the shipment and see what we're dealing with. If we know what and where it is, then at least we have leverage if we're cornered. And if cell service comes back, we'll be able to tell the police where it is…or whatever agency deals with this kind of thing."

"It's usually ATF," he said. "Bureau of Alcohol, Tobacco, Firearms and Explosives."

David frowned, but he didn't offer a different plan.

"And what happens after that?" he asked.

"I haven't figured that part out yet."

The sound of the snowmobile motor started, filling her with renewed dread. If she got out of this alive, she was never going to go near one of those things again.

"We can weave between these groups of trees until we get to the road," she said. "But when we cross it, there's no way he'll miss our tracks, and we'll be exposed."

"How's your ankle?" he asked.

It was a little sore, but there was nothing to do about it, so she waved off the question.

"I'm not so sure we make a good team, considering what happened back in my cabin," she muttered as she lifted her pack onto her back.

"We'd make a great team if you'd listen to me."

She looked up to glare at him, but she found a hint of a smile on his lips. And despite all that was happening around them, despite the danger they were still in, she smiled, too.

"I was thinking the same thing."

* * *

David had forgotten how this part of their relationship felt, the way they used to butt heads, each one
vying to be in charge, to do things their own way.
He loved this about her, the way she was so sure of
herself, so confident, not afraid to speak her mind.
But he couldn't ignore that this was also what had
led to her leaving him without discussion. Or maybe
Rain had foreseen the kind of arguments that would
come, both demanding things to go their way. Maybe
she'd known it would tear their relationship apart
from the inside.

If she hadn't left him, how else would it have
played out? He might have left firefighting, the only
job he had ever wanted, for her, but it would've hurt.
It would have been a scar in their relationship, one
that might never fully heal. He regretted the little
comment he'd made back in the house about her leaving him, and he wanted to apologize for it at some
point, when they had a little more time, but there
were more pressing matters.

He adjusted his pack on his back and secured
the clip around his waist again. "I say we lead him
across the road, away from the cabins, and head for
the summit pass, then for the cookout ledge if we
can lose him."

She nodded. "We'll have good cover from the
trees at first, but as we get higher on the mountain,
the trees thin out. We'll be more exposed."

"Let's hope we lose him by then," he said, though he wasn't counting on that.

"Ready?" she asked. "I'll go first."

David looked into her eyes as she blinked up at him, trying to ignore the warmth that hit him right in the chest. They were a team, imperfect but working together. It was temporary, and he had no idea yet how they'd make it beyond this threat, but despite the danger they were facing, he couldn't ignore how good it felt to be with her. He found himself giving a silent prayer. *Thank You for bringing us back together, just for a short while.* Then he gave her a lift of his chin. "Lead away."

The snowmobile engine was coming closer as Rain stuck her head out of the pines, then headed for the trees in the general direction of the road. They skied heading uphill at an angle. So far, he hadn't spotted the man. They reached the pair of pines and brushed through their green curtain, the needles scraping against his coat and his face. Rain continued out into the open, heading for the next stand.

The sun went down early in these parts, disappearing behind the mountains long before official sunset. The sky above was dark, gray clouds enveloping the mountain in a thick shroud. David wondered how long the snowstorm would hide them. The snowmobile motor was idling low, somewhere nearby. The guy had found their tracks. Rain disappeared into the next stand, and he followed as she headed out at a different angle. Would it slow their attacker down? There was a chance, but sooner or later, he was going to catch them.

Just before they disappeared into another mess of branches, David looked over his shoulder and caught a glimpse of something moving through the snowy veil. The headlight shone through the gray. The man was close.

Up ahead, Rain glanced over her shoulder at him. "We're at the road. We're going to have to sprint up this snowbank, across the road and over the other snowbank before we come to anything else we can use as a cover. You think we're far enough in front of him to be that exposed?"

The answer was no, but in situations like this, luck was really all they had.

"I think our chances aren't going to get any better," he said. "We need to try for it."

Rain didn't bother to answer. She turned and started across the wide expanse of the road in front of them. Watching her ski out into the open despite the danger filled him with a strange mix of fear and admiration. She had always talked about him walking into danger, like she couldn't decide whether or not it was a good thing, and he was starting to understand what was going through her mind. She looked fearless in the face of it. She started up the incline that the plows had created, taking it at an angle. David followed her, searching through the blowing snow for the trees on the other side, but all he saw was snow against the gray veil of the night.

The gunning of the snowmobile's motor was like a live wire hitting him, jolting his body into red alert. The sound was getting closer, and maybe only ten to fifteen feet behind them. As soon as the attacker made it around the clump of pines, he was going to see them. Rain made it up the incline, then switched to longer strides, gliding over the flat road, and he stayed close. The dark shadows of the trees were filtering through the blizzard. Just a few more meters and she'd ski up to safety. David's arms and legs were alive with adrenaline, pumping through him. He had a way of shutting off his thoughts in emergencies, but this time was different. He was aware of every sensation, every movement, every inch of terrain they still had to cross. Behind him, the snowmobile motor quieted to an idle. An icy wave of dread ran through him. The man had found them.

"Go," he shouted at Rain. David pushed aside his fear and focused on staying close, increasing the chances that he stayed between her and the man behind him. As she reached the far snowbank, a shot exploded, ringing through the hiss of the wind. Rain didn't even look back, just continued up the steep snowbank. Another burst of admiration ran through him, chased with a flicker of hope. This was the last stretch. David followed close behind. As she reached the top and disappeared down into the trees, a second shot came. His first thought was relief. Rain had made it out of sight before the assailant had gotten another shot. With his body on overdrive, his muscles burning, it wasn't until he headed into the sea of branches that he realized what that red-hot sensation in his arm was. He had been shot.

Chapter Seven

Rain was panting, her chest burning from the exertion, but they had a long, long way to go. She headed through the group of trees that lined the road, then made a sharp turn, hoping to throw the guy off. The headlight from the snowmobile flickered through the trees.

"You okay?" she asked over her shoulder.

He muttered something, but the wind carried away his voice.

"What?"

"I'm fine. Keep going."

She spotted their next cover and took off for the stand of trees as the engine of the snowmobile roared back to life. They were making progress, but they had quite a distance to go before they reached the summit. This guy was far too close right now. Navigating the road and hills the snowplow had built all winter would slow him down a bit, but after that, their pursuer was going to close in on them quickly. As they climbed, fewer trees had their lowest branches. The canopy was higher up, closer to the sun, leaving the forest floor more open. All they'd have for cover was the storm.

But here they were still low enough to hide in the trees. She had to use that to their advantage. They could double back from one of these tree stands, then head in a different direction. The snowmobile engine revved, like the guy was trying to go up the snowbank, and she knew it would be there soon. They came to a large clump of firs, four of them, with big long branches. She stopped in the middle of them and turned back to David.

"Wait here. I'm going to make tracks over to another stand, then double back. I'm hoping to buy us some time."

Rain fully expected an argument from him or maybe some sort of demand that he be the one to do it, but he just nodded. It was a little strange, but this wasn't the time to parse the leftover dynamics of their relationship, so she took her win and headed out into the open. She sprinted to a stand not far from them, then once she was between the trees, she turned her skis and headed back. When she returned to the clump of trees, David said nothing. His jaw was tense, and his mouth turned down into a frown. He didn't look happy with their situation.

"The plan is to stay inside these trees," she said.

"Let's hope he follows my trail to the next stand. If he does, we take off."

David nodded. There was an expression on his face that she couldn't read, but he didn't object to her plan, so she pointed her skis in a different direction from where they'd come in and from the one she'd gone out. She stopped behind a cover of branches, the snow tumbling down on her. Better cover, she supposed, so she didn't shake it off. David came up next to her, waiting. The snowmobile's motor came closer, buzzing on low as the rider navigated through the blowing wind. The snow was coming down hard, burying everything in new layers of white, but it wasn't enough to hide their tracks. Still, the visibility was poor. That was working on their side. She was thankful for any small advantage.

Rain pressed herself inside the trees, praying that the white of her jacket camouflaged her, praying that the headlight didn't shine directly on them. Her muscles were burning, and she was sweating. The moment she started to cool, that could spell disaster. She was going to need to stop somewhere and take off her inner layer if they ever made it to the cookout ledge. But that seemed so far away right now.

She was in decent shape, but after skiing all afternoon, she had probably burned through all the food she'd eaten and then some. Her body was running on pure adrenaline. Beside her, David stood motionless. Something felt off with them. The David she knew would be assessing their plan, going over it with her, figuring out how to navigate these next steps, but he was silent.

Rain turned to him. His jaw was clenched, and the little she could see of his brow under his hat was furrowed with tension.

"We've got a long way to go before we get to the pass," she said.

He gave a tilt of assent with his head, nothing more, so she continued.

"I think if we head up in this direction, we'll hit a few of those boulders." She pointed into the darkness. "They will give us some cover."

Still nothing, just a little nod. Maybe this was a new side of David, one she didn't know about. After all, a lot could change in five years. But a new thought dawned on her. Maybe David was regretting coming for her. After all, if she hadn't called him, he would be at his cabin with Isabel, making food and relaxing instead of out on this mountainside, running away from a man who had already shot at them six times. His regrets shouldn't be a surprise, considering his earlier comment about leaving him. She'd dragged him into her mess, and they were stuck in this together. But they were going to have to save his regrets for later.

The snowmobile came close, following the path they'd come from, tracing their ski tracks into this stand of trees. Rain held still, her breaths coming hard. The snowmobile circled, its light flashing between the trees. Her nerves were fraying. What if her plan to buy some time only got them caught? Her legs started to waver, and she grabbed on to David's sleeve, desperately trying not to tumble over into the snow. David's hand was there, and then his arm came around her.

"Are you all right?" he asked above the wind and the motor.

She nodded. "Just nerves. But I think I need to stop for food soon."

"We'll do that if we can get a little distance," he said, sounding more like his old self.

"If we think he's following my tracks to the next stand, we need to go," she said. "We can try to sprint to the boulder."

"I'll lead," he said. "The wind is going to be brutal."

Before she could respond, the headlight flashed in their direction. She stilled, taking comfort in the feeling of David's arm around her. She closed her eyes, praying for their safety, praying for *David's* safety. He didn't deserve any of this, but he was helping her anyway. She knew he wouldn't leave her until this was over. That gave her a burst of determination. The light shifted as the guy navigated around the trees, and then the snowmobile was moving away from them. It worked. The guy was moving onto the next set of trees behind them. *Thank You.* She opened her eyes, ready to face the storm.

"Let's go," he said.

Rain wrapped her hand around the pole handle and pushed off through the branches, following in David's tracks as he blazed a trail through the deep snow. Nightfall usually brought new gusts of wind, and tonight was no exception. As they came off the road from her house, the wind had come from the side, but they were now facing north, right into it. Large flakes of snow hit her face. Uphill and against the wind was a struggle, even with David in front of her to block some of the gusts. The new burst of energy she'd felt back in the trees was fading fast. Rain ducked her head and pushed on, moving one foot in front of another, trying not to lose the progress she was making. There was no other choice but to go on.

She lifted her head for signs of the boulders they were aiming for. There were a handful of them, spread out along the incline, enough to be forgiving of their blind navigation as long as they were headed in the right general direction. The narrow alleys between the rocks had been a favorite hiding place when they were kids. Rain noted that David was going at a pace she could keep up with. He must be holding back for her, and for that she was grateful.

She tucked her head against the wind, focusing on the tracks in front of her. The snowmobile's motor had mostly disappeared, so it was hard to hear how close their attacker was over the wind. She pushed on, telling herself it wasn't far, that she could do this. She told herself that God was watching them, guiding them, even if it didn't feel that way. She told herself that even if it was hard to understand God's plan, even if sometimes she doubted that there even was one, it couldn't be David's fate to die out here on this mountain. The thought pushed her forward. And despite all her doubts, she clung to that idea, repeating it in her head.

The next time Rain looked up, she caught a glimpse of the shadowy face of a boulder looming in front of them. They were almost there. Her hope had gotten her through this.

David must have seen their destination, too, because he sped up a little, pointing them to higher ground and into the little pathway between two of the boulders. As she came closer, the wind died down, the tall rocks protecting them a little. David led them through the narrow passageway. The boulders were mostly covered in snow except at the steepest parts, where the granite remained bare. They wouldn't be visible immediately if the man came this way. They had a bit of time, not much, but a bit. Rain bent over, her breaths heavy and coming one on top of the other, as she struggled to even them out.

She took one last deep breath and returned to standing. Next to her, David rested his back against the side of the boulder, not moving at all. Something was wrong. Her mind jogged back a few minutes before, when she was searching for the row of boulders,

and she caught a detail her mind had not registered
the first time around. David hadn't been using his
left arm to ski. She had been too busy struggling to
think about what that meant, but now it all clicked.
He was injured. That was why he'd been so quiet.
She moved forward to get a better look at him. A
small patch of red was seeping out from behind his
arm onto the snow. Everything came together in that
moment, sharp and painful and certain. David had
been shot. He was bleeding, and he hadn't said a
word about it.

There was a difference between fear and being
frightened, at least in David's mind. Fear was an
idea, something he could hold at a distance, exam-
ine and use to his advantage. It could help him assess
the dangers and how best to deal with them. Being
frightened was something different. That came with
a hint of panic, a scattering of his thoughts instead
of a sharpening of them. And in those differences
was where the most danger lay. David wasn't frightened for his own injury. It was the question that kept
running through his mind: How long could he protect Rain? This one was followed by an even more
jarring thought. As a nurse, Rain would stop to care
for him, no matter how close the man was. Would
that be the reason they were caught?

David had been injured plenty of times before.
It came with the territory of being a firefighter. He

had been burned, hit with falling objects, and had suffered from extreme dehydration and exhaustion. One time, smoke inhalation had taken him under and Hakeem had pulled his unconscious body from the wreckage of the building. He didn't remember much about that time. But the burning sensation in his lungs had gone away, and at that time, he had been more focused on nursing his heartache than his lungs. But being shot in the middle of this chase through the blizzard was a new level of fright. What if his body broke down, and Rain suffered because of it?

Please, God. I can't let her down. She needs to be safe.

Rain's hands were resting on her thighs, her head hanging down, as she heaved in breaths. As the words of prayer came to him, she stood up and looked over at him. Her mouth turned down to a frown, so he straightened up. He had plenty of reserves in him. He opened his mouth to say something about getting something to eat, but she was staring at his injured arm.

"You're bleeding," she said, fear leaking into her voice. It was the reason he hadn't said anything. He wasn't going to hold them back. They were already at a disadvantage, with the man on a snowmobile and them on skis. David didn't want to distract her. They could take care of this when they were safely hidden.

"I need to look at your arm," she said.

He opened his mouth to say he could make it to the cookout ledge, but Rain gave a sharp shake of her head. Her mouth formed a firm, straight line of determination, and she whipped off her pack and began searching through it. This was no longer the woman who had walked away from him five years ago, with all the heaviness that came from those memories. This was the woman who had funneled the sorrow of her parents' deaths into the determination to save lives. She had contemplated following the path to be a doctor, knowing that it would come with more prestige and more money. And she had needed money. Still, she'd decided she wanted to be a nurse. It was the patient care that pushed her decision, the personal side of nursing, the connection that it brought.

Before her parents' death, she had been ambivalent about college. Not long after that funeral, he'd seen this determination rise, the resolve to bring good into a world that had taken so much from her. In truth, that was when he first began to believe, really believe deep down, in God. He had never thought too much about it, though he had gone to church with his family all his life. Sometimes the world was just too much to inspire belief in anything. But seeing her rise from the ashes of her devastating loss had hit him hard. It had changed things for him. That was a long time ago, and David had witnessed enough hardships in the world to make his faith waver. But seeing Rain like this, her determination increasing again despite everything that happened today... That moved something deep inside him.

Rain was holding a bandanna, the Swiss army knife and a pencil. He wasn't sure he wanted to know what she was planning to do with those, so David just held out his arm. He winced as she turned it gently, inspecting what she could see. She balanced her gloves on her pack and pulled the scissors out of the Swiss army knife, then began to cut a long slit up the arm of his jacket.

"This was a nice coat," he grumbled.

"Don't worry. I'll duct-tape it back together," she said with a hint of a smile, then glanced up. "I told you it might be useful."

Despite the cold air rushing in, under his layers, and the feeling that a hive of bees was stinging his arm, the corners of his mouth turned up.

She put away the scissors and peered at his arm. "I think it was a clean shot, just skimming the inside of your arm."

"Is that a good or a bad thing?"

"Depends, but I'm going to say good as of now. You made it this far, and you're still talking."

The snowmobile had been buzzing in the background, filtering through over the gusts of wind, and a faint light shone from around the side of the boulder.

"We don't have much time right here," she said, scrambling to take off her pack. She reached for the

bandanna. "I'm going to use this for a quick tourniquet, just to make sure the bullet didn't hit an artery."

She wound the bandanna around his arm, tied it,
then stuck the pencil under the material, using the
utensil to twist it, tightening it around his arm. When
she was satisfied, she looked up at him.

"I'm going to quickly check your pulse and ask you
a couple questions while we wait," she said, raising
her fingers to his throat.

There was an intimacy to this little gesture, and
for a moment, it felt like it was five years ago. Like
they were connected again. He blinked, taking in her
confidence, her competence. He'd always assumed
she was a great nurse, but it was different to see her
in action.

"What's your name?"

He raised his eyebrows, and she let out a little huff.

"Just answer."

"David Hernandez."

"Where are we?"

"Heading up toward Crystal Summit, farther and
farther from our warm cabins."

The corners of her mouth tilted up. "What year
is it?"

He looked at her, all traces of humor gone. "Seven
months after Brandon died."

In the years after her parents had died, she had
referred to time that way—eighteen months after
the crash, twenty-four, fifty. She'd talked about it a

lot, enough so he assumed she was doing the same with Brandon. By the way she was looking at him, nodding, he was pretty sure he'd guessed correctly.

"You're fine so far," she said after a moment, then began to unwind the pencil from the bandanna. His fingers tingled as she studied the wound from under the tourniquet, then let out a sigh. "No artery, as far as I can tell."

She tied the bandanna again, then pulled out the duct tape. "We'll do some mild compression over your jacket until we have time for more. It's not ideal, but it should stem the loss of blood until we get to the cookout ledge."

She said this all as she found the end of the tape and pulled it out, using it to close the hole in his jacket. The bandanna pressed tightly against his bicep, but not nearly as tightly as the tourniquet had.

"That actually feels a little better," he said, inspecting it with care.

"'Actually?'"

She thought he was doubting her skills? Not a chance. "I mean I didn't think there was anything you could do to make a gunshot wound feel better."

"I guess I learned something in nursing school," she said, but this time she was smiling a little.

"We have to go," he said.

"I need to check that you're not hit anywhere else," she said, inspecting his coat. "The bullet could have gone through your coat and into your side."

David was sure that wasn't the case, but he let

her check without comment. His senses kicked in as he waited, and the first thing he noticed was that he had started to cool down. It was a reminder of yet another danger out here. Hypothermia. The elements were just as much a threat as the guy chasing them, though the noise of the snowmobile was coming through louder above the wind. The guy was on their trail. They needed to get moving soon or they'd be trapped.

"From here to the summit pass is going to be a tough route, especially considering the low visibility," she said. "There's a good chance we'll hit the summit wall first, then follow it to the pass. But after we cross the pass, we'll be able to follow the boulders down to the cookout ledge."

David's brain was starting to function a little better now that his arm wasn't throbbing as badly.

"I could slow him down. I can wait here and lure him off his snowmobile, then attack him," he said. "I'm bigger than that guy, and if we're close enough, I can take him down."

She glared at him.

"Are you kidding me? You just got shot in the arm." She paused, then added, "We can't risk that."

There was a waver in her voice, an emotion he hadn't heard from her in so long. It was a bad idea to hope, but desperate times called for desperate measures, so he let himself linger on her words, on the emotion in her voice. He let himself hope she cared for him more than just as a patient, though he wasn't ready to think about why that mattered.

"Fine," he said. "The only other option is to sprint for the summit and try not to get shot."

As far as plans went, this was a pretty bad one, but they didn't have much other choice. Rain stuffed the medical supplies back into her pack, then swung it around to her back.

"I noticed you weren't using your left arm much when we were coming up," she said. "That's good. Try not to unless you need it."

"Not a problem." Just thinking about moving it made his arm burn. "Ready?"

"Ready."

They continued through the little path formed by the boulders. The wind whipped around the corner, and soon they were facing the open blizzard again. To the left the mountain sloped down, back to the safety of the cabins, and to the right was an uphill climb, toward the summit. With any luck, the man would try to find their path heading down the hill, back toward safety. With any luck, that would give them a head start. And as he pushed off with his right pole, heading uphill, a thought came to him that gave him a little push forward.

Maybe we don't make such a bad team.

Chapter Eight

When they skied from the stand of pines to the boulders, Rain had kept her head down, worrying about her own endurance. Now she was worried about David's, too. His black jacket masked the extent of his blood loss, and as she worked her way up the hill, she wondered if she had made a mistake in simply settling for a compression rather than taking the time to inspect his wound. But that choice was gone, so she focused on what she had in her backpack that she could use to triage a gunshot wound. He needed a hospital or at least some sort of medical facility. The closest thing was the urgent care center in Clover Valley, but she and David were heading into the mountains, farther and farther away from civilization. With his years in the volunteer search and rescue team, maybe David was coming up with a plan…though it didn't seem like he was in much condition to do a lot of thinking right now.

Rain pushed her skis forward, gliding through the tracks that David had set. Her poles were sinking too deeply to get much traction, making the uphill journey even more difficult. David's shape was a blur of shadowy darkness ahead, his shoulders hunched against the wind as he pushed forward. She followed, skiing into the darkness that was settling on the mountainside. At least that was working in their favor. Through the wind, the snowmobile revved, announcing itself. Out of the corner of her eye, she caught flashes from the headlights as it bounded over the snow-covered landscape. Sooner or later, this guy would be back on their trail. If this plan went perfectly, they'd hit the summit pass and start down before the man reached them. But how often did plans go perfectly?

Up ahead, David stopped, and she had a moment of panic. What was he doing?

David was looking at the ground, and she had a pang of fear that he was going to collapse, but then he began again, steadily making his way through the snow. She continued, but as she approached the spot where he had stopped, she saw what he'd been looking at. Perpendicular to the path they were forging was another set of tracks, but this one wasn't human. It was narrow and deep and recent, judging from the little snow that had settled on top of it. Rain paused, inspecting it. It wasn't made by deer. The prints were too big and too shallow. She took one more look and then continued after David, turning the puzzle over in her mind as she took each arduous step. Bears hibernated at this time of the year, and the path was too narrow for one anyway. Mountain lions and lynx roamed these parts, but the big cats tended to travel alone. The path they had passed had far too many prints to belong to a solitary animal. The same logic applied to coyotes, on the off chance one had come out of hibernation. Truthfully, the path looked most like something Maple and her friends would make. She felt a burst of warmth as she thought of Maple, sitting in the Hernandez living room, maybe cuddling on the floor next to Isabel. At least they were safe right now.

Maybe someone's lost dogs were wandering on the mountainside? It wasn't out of the question, considering her own dog had made a similar journey yesterday, but this wasn't just a dog or two. It would have had to be a pack of them. The word *pack* triggered another possibility in her mind. Wolves. Weren't wolves extinct in California? She'd never heard of any around here, and this area was pretty good about keeping residents up-to-date about animal sightings. She would've heard if there were wolves known to be roaming this area…wouldn't she? Then again, she hadn't been up to Crystal Lake since last spring. A lot could have happened in a year. She knew that as well as anyone.

Her body was heating up again. She tugged at the

zipper of her jacket, pulling it down a little, letting the cool air leak inside. The relief gave her another burst of energy, for which she was grateful. Any boost helped. The sound of the engine had flagged for a bit, but now it was back. She glanced over her shoulder and saw the dim glow of the spotlight coming directly toward them. But the farther they went, the slower they were moving. Her energy was flagging, and David seemed to be feeling the storm, too. The trees were starting to disappear, which meant they were reaching the tree line. How far could they be from the summit pass? She looked out into the blur of snow and wind, but she couldn't see anything familiar to orient herself. They must be close... Unless they had gotten off course. In fact, the longer they went, the more the sinking feeling of dread set in.

Then, up ahead, Rain spotted a tall, shadowy mass rising up like a wall in front of them. It was the towering peak of Crystal Summit, where the forest turned to bare stone. The mountain rose up between the ledge and the summit pass, so the fact that they were headed straight for it meant they had gotten off course. They were approaching a wall of stone, with nowhere to hide. As soon as the guy on the snowmobile reached them, they would be trapped.

She wanted to yell to David, to warn him, but she was breathing too hard to get out much sound over the bellow of the wind. After a few more strides,

David seemed to notice the problem and turned to the north, pointing them in the direction of where the pass should be. But the motor from the snowmobile was getting louder, and when she looked over her shoulder, the headlight had gotten much brighter. They were racing against the clock, and Rain was starting to think that they weren't winning.

But there was nothing to do except focus. David was moving ahead of her, blazing a trail through the deep snow, and she scanned the shadow of the mountain for a break.

Just focus on the pass. Don't look back.

The dark wall of rock sloped down, and after that, it was only snow. *Yes.* Almost there. But the sound of the motor rang in her ears, loud and insistent. The man was right behind them, and the pass was right in front of them. David turned the corner, aiming them toward the flat, narrow path that led to the other side of the mountain.

Keep going. You can do this.

But as the words ran through her head, the snowmobile's engine stopped next to her. When she glanced to the side, the guy was staring at her with a look of triumph.

"Stop," he called.

David looked over his shoulder, and she silently begged him to stop. The man already had shown he was willing to use the gun. David seemed to be thinking along the same lines because he stopped and looked over his shoulder, first at the man and then at Rain. He was probably making the assessment she already had: they were trapped.

The guy pulled out his gun and waved it between the two of them. "This ends here."

They were so close to crossing the pass, but that didn't matter. When it came to life and death, close to safe didn't count. David had been close to reaching Hakeem that day, close to the room where his best friend had been trapped, but in the end, the distance he'd gained didn't matter. All that mattered to him and to Angela, all that mattered to their team, was that Hakeem hadn't survived. David had hoped never to be in this situation again, and he had spent the last two years with this weight on his shoulders. But he was right back here again, the stakes unbearably high. This was Rain, and he couldn't deny any longer that the feelings he'd had for her, the ones he had tried so hard not to think about, were still there, as strong as ever. Despite the fact that they'd been apart for five years, the thought of losing her was too much, no matter what happened between them. This day was a disaster in every way.

Rain was looking between him and the man, her eyes wide with fear. He had to get her away from that gun.

"I'm giving you one more chance," the man called above the wind. "You have our property. All you need to do is lead me to it. Once we've made the exchange, we can go our separate ways."

Anger coursed through his voice, as if he had lost patience with this long ago. But so had David. He knew better than to believe that this would be so simple, and he was sure Rain did, too. But a gun was moving back and forth between her and David. This wasn't about trust or belief. This was about survival. Rain didn't answer, and David could see the man was getting angrier. He was focusing all his words and attention on Rain, just glancing at David from time to time to make sure he wasn't moving.

"You have what I need," said the man, then gestured to David. "This guy has nothing I want."

Rain had told him the same thing earlier, but her eyes widened at the guy's words. They made the threat feel much more real.

"If you shoot him right now, there is no chance I will ever get you what you want."

David had to admire how strong she sounded, in the face of all the danger.

But the man's expression relaxed a little, like this was what he had been waiting to hear. Like she was confirming his suspicions.

"Now we're understanding each other," he said, and David could've sworn there was a hint of a smile on his lips.

The longer they stood here, the more uneasy David grew. He glanced at Rain. Her eyes were filled with fear, despite the firmness he'd heard in her voice.

"After you let him go safely, I'll come with you," she said.

The words jabbed in his gut.

"No, Rain," he growled. "This isn't going to go well for either of us."

She had to know that the moment she showed him to the stash, he would need to get rid of her. She had to know that going with him meant putting herself at his mercy. She couldn't go back to his trailer, even if his wife and baby were there. For plenty of people, empathy didn't extend beyond their own family. This man wouldn't spare her.

"Please, David," she said. "I can't put you in danger like this. And your arm… You need to take care of it."

He barely heard the soft tone of her voice over the wind and the idle of the motor, but it hit him in another swift jab. Was she confident that he would think of something to help her, or was she really sacrificing herself for him? It didn't matter. After all their years apart, this couldn't be where they went separate ways. It wouldn't be. Because there was no chance David would allow her to be taken away by a weapons trafficker.

A plan was forming in his mind, risky under any conditions and even riskier with one arm wounded. But there was no use thinking about the odds right now.

"Anything you need from me," he said to her, "I'll do it."

The words were the absolute truth, and they resonated deep down in David. Her expression softened,
as if she, too, were feeling the full weight of what he
was saying.

The man on the snowmobile looked triumphant
as Rain began to sidestep over to the snowmobile on
her skis. David turned around and followed.

"Don't come any closer," said the man, aiming a
gun straight at him.

"Her ankle is injured," said David. "She's going
to need help with her skis. Unless you are planning
to get off and help her."

The man looked uncertainly from one of them to
the other. David glanced at Rain, and her eyes were
frightened again.

Trust me. He tried to convey this silently, praying
that she would understand.

David lifted his hands in surrender, his wounded
arm burning at the movement. "You know neither
of us is armed. We would have shot at you long before if we were. And you hit my left arm when I was
crossing the road. I'm not a threat."

The man sized him up, and David was sure he
was noting David's larger size. He hoped the man
also noted the duct tape around his arm, which cor-
roborated his story. They all paused there in a frozen
tableau, as the snow blew against them.

Finally, the guy gave a little nod. "You can help
her. But no sudden moves."

Rain was glaring at him. She already had told him

twice that her ankle was fine, so she knew he was planning something. He just prayed she would trust him to try.

They silently moved over toward the snowmobile, as the man pointed the gun at David.

Forget this is Rain. Focus on this like it is any other rescue.

David took a deep breath and allowed the scene to play out in his mind, looking at the snowmobile. That was the key. He had to get as close as possible for this to work. It was a challenge, getting through the snow like this. David reached the snowmobile and squatted, reaching for her binding. He pretended to fumble with it a little as he calculated the distance between him and the gun. The guy had moved back in his seat a little, but there was no way to avoid it. He was within reach. It was now or never.

David shifted closer, like he was adjusting his stance, and he lifted his right arm up and gave the man's hand a swift blow. The gun went off as David watched it fly out of the man's hand and land somewhere downhill in the snow. He had just bought them a minute or two of time. With any luck, that would be enough.

He gave the man a hard shove, pushing him off his seat, into the deep snow. David whipped around and looked at Rain. "Are you hurt?"

"N-no." She looked shocked, like she was registering what had happened these last few minutes.

Thank You, Lord.

"Then let's go."

He didn't wait for her to answer. David grabbed his poles, and the burning sensation in his left arm flared. Any bleeding that had subsided probably was flowing again, but there were more important things, like getting over the pass with Rain.

He started for it, just a few yards away. The man yelled something, but David couldn't hear what it was over the wind. Their attacker likely was scrambling back on the snowmobile. Now was the last possible place David's plan could fail. If the man was carrying two guns, David was a dead man. So he had to believe the man wasn't. He had to have faith.

Chapter Nine

Rain raced through the snow. Just a few more yards and they would be on the pass. Just a few more yards and they would no longer be direct targets. The snowmobile's motor sped up, then slowed. The guy likely was looking in the snow for the gun. Once he found it, he'd be on their tail again. Was this guy going to take the snowmobile down the steeper side of the mountain? They were about to find out.

A thin cloud of new snow blew over the summit, settling against the tall granite rocks and making the pass into a slope. Some of the snow blew past them, down the other side, but the snow that did settle was packed hard. At least that meant she could get good leverage with her poles.

Rain's arms ached as she pushed against the wind, across the summit pass, her skis gliding over the drifts of snow and scraping against the ice below. The snow whipped through the air and pelted the side of her face. She glanced back at David. His head was bent against the wind, and he was using both arms to push himself forward. She wanted to yell that he shouldn't be using his wounded arm, but even if he could hear her over the wind, it wouldn't matter. David would do whatever it took to make sure they were safe, even at the expense of himself. She had gone over this thought many times, and she hadn't made peace with it. The knowledge was an ache inside, growing, the way it had in the past. But this wasn't the past, and she and David weren't together, so Rain pushed that thought away and focused on the present. They needed to get to the cookout ledge without this guy following them. It was their best chance for cover at this point, and she needed to find out what Brandon was hiding there. Even if what they found might break her heart.

The pass was a long, narrow ledge that curved around between the peaks of Crystal Summit. On the one side was a tall wall of granite, and on the other was a precipitous drop-off. Rain stuck as close to the bare rocks as she could, but the wind whipped in her eyes. She couldn't see the edge of the drop-off. It was just a blur of snow, but she knew what was down there: a cliff too far down for anyone to survive. If the man on the snowmobile followed them over the pass, he would face the same conditions. At least that was working for them.

Her ski skittered over the icy snow, jarring her out of her thoughts. She was sliding, moving dangerously down the slope, toward the cliff. She scrambled, her skis scraping against the snow as she struggled to get her feet under her. Through the blizzard, she could make out the edge of the cliff, which was coming closer.

"Rain!" David's voice cut through the wind.

She leaned uphill and brought down her knees, but she was still sliding. Rain gulped in a breath as she went into emergency mode. It was all ice here, close to the edge. Before she could think better of it, she looked down. The tips of her skis dangled into the snowy abyss. Her heart raced faster. She attacked the icy snow hard with the top of her pole. Again. On the third jab, the snowy crust cracked. *Thank You.* She tried with the other hand, pounding the handle of her pole until it broke through, too. Her slow slide came to a stop.

Her heart was pounding in her ears, but she didn't have time to be afraid. She dragged her knees under her, scrambling up the slope, back toward safety. Rain blew out a long breath. That was close. She didn't let herself look back. Instead, she looked up at David. Through the blowing snow, she could see his mouth set in a grim line. She gave him a little nod and pulled herself to her feet.

She started forward, sticking close to the rock face, testing for ice on each stride. Now that she was moving at a moderate pace, she noticed more animal tracks underneath her skis, partly covered by the blowing snow. She and David weren't the first to cross the summit pass tonight.

They wound around the mountain, the sound of the snowmobile dimming behind the walls of granite. But the man would be on their tail soon, so she focused all her thoughts forward. She pushed, gliding over the windswept snowbanks until the pass opened up, and the hill began its descent. The terrain on this side of the mountain was different, steeper, with jagged rocks that stuck out.

When they were kids, she, Brandon, David and Isabel would ski this side like an obstacle course, dodging trees and rocks while pushing each other to go faster. The phone reception on this side was terrible, so they had to convince one of their parents to pick them up on the road a couple miles down, to drive them home.

David headed downhill, following the side of the summit peaks closely. After a few turns, she spotted tracks again. The animals already had navigated a path down. Her parents had taught them how to use the animal runs, how to take note of the markers so they didn't get lost in the forest, and she, David, Brandon and Isabel had found a new freedom in their explorations. But this wasn't deer that would scatter the moment they scented humans. This was something else, and following the path meant there was a chance they would find out exactly what that something else was.

She stopped next to the animal tracks and waited for David to catch up. "What do you think? Wolves?"

"I was wondering the same thing."

His expression was strained, and her heart gave a thump of fear. He looked tired. She needed to get a peek at his arm. They needed to stop soon.

As they traced the edge of the mountain, she spotted a dark opening at the base. A cave. The caves were scattered along the base of the summit peaks, some dead ends, some leading to other caves, human-sized or smaller. One of them led to the cookout ledge.

"David," she called, but the howl of the wind swallowed her voice. She tried again. "David."

He came to a stop, and Rain skied next to him. "He's going to follow our tracks. I think we should cut through the caves."

"You sure?" David tilted his head. Was he remembering the way she'd refused to explore the tunnels, waiting outside, where she could breathe easier?

But she couldn't let her fears rule her, so she added, "It would be hard for the guy to follow us. And I have to go in there to know for sure about Brandon…"

David was quiet for a bit, then frowned. "Do you remember which ones to take?"

"I think so." She hoped so. Otherwise they'd be trapped. She needed to get this right. For both of their sakes.

David had had enough close calls today to last him a lifetime, and they were still far from safety. He didn't want to think about what had happened back at the pass as Rain slid toward the precipice. For the first time, he had frozen in the face of danger as fear for her had flooded him. And all he could think of was this: They had both suffered enough, hadn't they?

Though David knew that the world didn't work this way, he prayed for their safety together. And in that prayer was a spark of hope he had thought had died. Hope was a dangerous thing—so light and magical, but ultimately at the mercy of the fickle winds of life. The hope that had brought him closer to her once had been irreparably damaged, hadn't it?

Rain skied in front of him, stopping to search in the dark hollows of rock as they made their way along the granite walls that formed the Crystal Summit. They were moving slower now, and David was grateful for that. The adrenaline of the confrontation with the man on the snowmobile was waning, and his arm needed attention. And a rest. But he was wary of the path Rain had chosen for them. She hated tight spaces. More than once, when they were exploring this area, he'd talked her through a tight space when she was verging on hyperventilation. But this was her choice, and he needed to try to trust her judgment… At least about this.

Rain picked her way around a set of boulders, then headed back in toward an opening just as dark as the last one. She stopped underneath a ledge where the snow ended and the cave began.

"This is it," she said, then threw a glance in his direction. "I'm almost sure."

"You lead." He tried to ignore the wariness that echoed through him.

She took off her skis, and he did the same, attempting to avoid using his injured arm. Rain pulled a rope out of her backpack and tied it around all four skis with a knot near the tips and another at the ends, forming a long strap that she used to lift them.

"I'll carry that," he said, his instinct to carry whatever load he faced outweighing his common sense.

She frowned at him. "We can take turns. I'll go first."

Despite the burn of his arm and the danger around them, he smiled. "Are you managing me?"

"Maybe." When she looked up from rummaging further through her backpack, she was smiling, too.

They started into the cave, trudging through the last of the snow and into the dark abyss. His eyes were slow to adjust, and the granite walls were filled with shadows. Rain clicked on a tiny penlight, the kind doctors used to check patients' pupils, and it confirmed what his memories told him: the cave was narrowing. The farther they walked, the more tension radiated from Rain. Were the confines of the cave rattling her nerves, or was it the possibility of being trapped at the back of this cave when the man on the snowmobile traced their tracks? His instincts told him to do something to protect her, to ease her worries, but he was trying to avoid that feeling. He'd do for her what he'd do for anyone else. He'd made peace with this, hadn't he?

After Hakeem's death, the full weight of the risks of fighting fires had hit him. Angela's ache for her husband was painful to watch, and the money from Hakeem's life insurance wouldn't last forever. David and the rest of the team had been there to support her, but he understood Angela's point: they couldn't do that forever. She needed to figure out how she and baby Malik would survive, so she'd gently but firmly distanced herself from them. David swallowed the grief he felt each time he thought of Angela, struggling as a single mother, and Malik, who would not remember his father. He didn't want to ever put someone through that kind of grief. His job was dangerous, but it saved people's lives. Deep down, he knew it was the work he was meant to do. But it came at a risk to those close to him, a risk that had become all too real this last year. So he had promised himself he wouldn't put someone in Angela's position, and he was willing to accept the loneliness that came from that decision.

David was startled out of his thoughts as Rain rounded a boulder and came to a stop against an impenetrable wall of granite. His heart jumped in his chest as he took in her frown. Had she taken a wrong turn? Were they trapped at the back of this cave? He wasn't in top form right now, and the burning sensation in his arm was hard to ignore, but the drive to protect was pumping a fresh wave of adrenaline through him. *I'll get her out of this, any way I can.* The intensity of the thought surprised him, and he pushed it away and focused on what was right in front of him.

"Do you want the good news or the bad news first?" she asked.

David knew he should take the bad news first, but after thinking about Angela, Malik and the pain of their loss, he needed a moment to prepare himself.

"The good."

"We are on the right path."

He glanced at what looked like a dead end in front of them. It seemed impossible, but that little balloon of hope expanded inside, daring him to believe that somehow there was a way out of this. "What's the bad?"

"The passageway is even smaller than I remembered."

Chapter Ten

It was all coming back to her, the memories that she had buried deeply. Each effort to put her most difficult memories of Brandon behind her was an act of self-preservation that had gotten her through the last seven months. But the recollections were now fresh again, as if she were searching these caves for Brandon and not just this awful legacy he'd left behind. She thought of the nights her brother had spent here and the dread each time that maybe she wouldn't find him. Whenever Brandon disappeared to stay here, her claustrophobia had warred with her worries. Each time she'd feared, what if her brother never came back this time? She'd forced herself to search everywhere, even in the tunnels, until she found him.

Rain remembered the tunnel in front of her. From where David was standing, it looked like a dead end, but she could see what David couldn't: a passageway that connected this one to the one on the cookout ledge. It had been too small for her comfort in the summertime, but with the extra bulk of her jacket and her backpack, now it felt like the stuff of nightmares.

Rain was trying hard not to think about that and to focus on the other challenges in front of them. "The passage is small, so we'll need to wrap all our gear on the skis and pull it through." She glanced at his arm. "I should take a look at your wound before we do this."

"Let's wait until we're through."

He looked tired, and if it were five years ago, she would have pressed him. But it wasn't five years ago, and she no longer had the right to pry into his feelings, so she nodded and turned to the pile of skis she had laid on the wet floor of the cave. She placed her poles on top of it, then her backpack, and David did the same. After securing them with rope, she squatted to shine her light through the tunnel's entrance.

"No wolves or bears that I can see." She said it in a joking voice, but David frowned at her.

"I should go first."

"Not a chance," she said quickly.

"You hate small spaces."

She flashed him a tight grin. "I can handle it."

Rain got down on her knees and looped the ski rope over her shoulder. The trick was to think about only what was in front of her. It was why she'd loved the emergency room. The work focused her, pulled her into the present, the place where she had the power to help, to make a difference.

The little tunnel echoed with the rub of her winter clothes and the scrape of the skis on the stone floor. The passage's ceiling was getting lower, and her breaths came more rapidly. What if she got trapped in here? What if California had one of its famous earthquakes, and the rock above came…

Rain's breaths were now coming in fast pants. She squeezed her eyes shut and drew a longer, shaky inhale.

"Rain?" David's voice rebounded through the little space, surrounding her. "Are you all right?"

"I don't even know how to answer that."

He gave a wry little laugh that echoed through the cave and warmed her just a little. And with it came a hint of lightness, a spark of relief. Her chest opened a little, and her breaths calmed. There was so much comfort in his voice, and there was a comfort in knowing he was holding up, too.

"I'll be okay," she added after a long, steady gulp of air.

The tunnel curved as she brought her hand down to move forward, and then she saw it: a dim glow of daylight. They were getting close to the next cave.

"Not far," she whispered to herself.

She crawled forward, one knee, then the other, dragging the skis as gently as she could, until the mouth of the tunnel widened. She stopped at the entry to the chamber and pulled out her penlight to check for movement.

The place was as she remembered it, squat and wide, with a smooth floor where Brandon used to sleep. But as she scanned the rest of the cave, her heart jumped. Something was in the back, a dark lump.

David crawled out next to her, balancing on his good arm.

"Do you think that's the…?" She let her voice trail off and focused her light on the dark shape. She almost wished it were an animal instead of the evidence of Brandon's path downhill. Still, there was a little part of her that still hoped that somehow this was all a mistake, that she would find something different. That somehow she wouldn't have to confront the hardest pieces of her past.

Rain abandoned the bundle of skis and approached the lump in the corner. A tarp was spread across something… David was behind her, but he was silent, following her lead. She stopped in front of the heap and reached down to lift a corner of the tarp. The first thing she saw was a wooden crate, long and flat. Her stomach twisted as she raised the tarp farther, uncovering more and more crates. David came up next to her and used his pocketknife to pry open the lid of the top one. Guns. Not hunting rifles but assault rifles. She dropped the corner and looked away, swallowing the lump in her throat. She'd known this was coming, but it didn't hurt any less.

"Now we know for sure," she said, her voice wobbling.

She could feel David's presence behind her, sympathy radiating from him. His hand rested on her shoulders. Was he going to pull her closer, take her into his arms the way he had back at the cabin? Part of her wanted that, to feel the safety of his embrace, but nothing about this felt safe. Not the cave, and not wanting to take comfort in David.

"I should take a look at your arm," she said, trying to channel her professional side.

David nodded and took a seat on the floor next to the backpack. She knelt by him to inspect the place she'd patched up. The duct tape seemed to be holding the coat together, and she didn't see signs of more bleeding.

"How are you feeling?"

"Tired but okay."

"You're doing well for someone with a bullet wound," she said, giving him a pointed look. "Are you sure you're not going to pass out on me?"

He gave her a little smile. "Not yet."

"I'm going to start by taking your pulse." She pulled off her gloves and took out her phone. She set the timer for a minute, laid two fingers against the warm skin on his neck, ignoring the jump of her own heart when she did, and tried as hard as she could to count. She blocked out how close they were, how much she had missed this nearness to him. She tried not to stare at his cheekbones, high and pronounced, and the warm brown of his skin, but she couldn't help it. This was David.

The timer went off, startling him just as much as it had her.

"Seventy-two beats per minute," she said. "Not bad."

"It's high for me."

"Noted. I'm going to look at your arm now, okay?"

He nodded. She pulled out the first aid kit and found the scissors, then began to cut open his jacket again, trying to follow the same lines she had used before. The blood had seeped into the bandanna around the wound.

Rain wasn't prepared for the way she startled when she caught sight of it. Anyone who worked in an ER had a way of hardening themselves. It had taken her a while to learn the skill, and she wasn't always successful, so she'd learned to deal with the pain of seeing so much suffering. But it was one thing to detach herself when faced with a stranger's injuries, and entirely another to remain so while treating the man she used to love. Her instincts were failing her, and emotions flooded in. She'd treated gunshot wounds in the ER, but she couldn't trust herself to make the right decisions, to remember the right things to do when she was scared. But David had no other options. He was depending on her, which was the last thing either of them wanted.

It was best to bandage him up and get him to the ER as soon as possible. And keep her mind off the worst-case scenarios that were scrolling through her mind.

"Tell me about your job these days," she said.

He glanced at her, as if he was unsure if she was serious.

"It'll keep my mind occupied," she added.

He nodded. "It's not so different from what it was five years ago. Sometimes there's a lot of action, and other days I do more waiting around."

"What's the most memorable thing that's happened lately?"

She worked quickly as he considered her question, stuffing gauze on the wound. Holding the pieces in place, she threaded the bandanna around his arm, directly against his skin.

"I delivered a baby," he said with a little smile. "That was definitely memorable."

Rain paused. "Really?"

He nodded. "Our truck got to the house before the ambulance, and the baby didn't want to wait."

As she sealed his coat with duct tape, David told her about the woman, stuck at home without a car, and the fear she'd experienced when she realized she was having the baby in her living room. But he also talked about her joy.

She finished sealing his jacket and put the first aid equipment back in her bag.

"You were meant to do this job," she said quietly as she settled against the cave wall next to him.

"I think I was," he said. "But it's not all happy endings, and that's hard to leave behind every day."

She nodded. "That's why I left the ER."

"Do you miss it?"

"A lot." Every day, in fact. "It felt like I was doing something important. Something for others."

"You still are."

"But it doesn't feel the same."

Rain knew he understood because he was the same as she was. It was what had brought them together and what pulled them apart.

"I agree, but it comes with a price," he said after a while. "After Hakeem died, I decided I couldn't take that risk."

"You don't want to have a family anymore?" She turned to him in surprise. David, who had always wanted a big family at the center of his life, had given up that future?

He didn't answer right away, and in that pause, she sensed his hesitation. Had he given up one dream for another?

"Maybe in the future," he said, "but I'm not counting on it."

The wind whipped at the entrance to the cave as

the snow piled higher. Soon they'd need to dig their way out.

"We're getting snowed in here," he said.

"I'd say we should stay here until it's over, but you really need to get to the Clover Valley clinic and have someone look at your arm." Rain stifled a yawn.

"But first I could use a rest," he said.

The exhaustion of the last few hours was settling into her limbs, begging her to sit for just a little longer.

"Just for a bit," she said and rested her head against his shoulder. "I'll set my alarm to make sure we're not out for too long."

He let out a sigh that sounded like relief, and she drifted off to the sound of his steady breaths.

David awoke in a foggy haze to the beep of an alarm. Rain was lying on his shoulder, still asleep, and it took a moment to realize that he wasn't dreaming. She really was there, beside him. His brain was a little bleary, and his arm was starting to feel numb, which he knew wasn't a good sign. Still, part of him didn't want to wake Rain. He didn't want this moment to end.

David also knew he shouldn't be thinking this way, so he gave her a little shake. "Time to get moving."

She sat up and blinked at him, like she was just as disoriented as he was. Then she reached for the phone to turn it off.

"We should head back to the cabin and get—" Her voice cut off as she sat up, rigid. "Did you hear that?"

"Hear what?"

He held still, listening to the wind, when he heard the sound. A scraping of something against rock, maybe plastic? Was the man with the gun nearby? If he was, the alarm had just given them away. David blamed the exhaustion for not having thought through that possibility, but now it was too late.

"If that's our guy, we need to move," said Rain, scrambling to her feet. "Quickly."

She was up and gathering their packs and skis before her words sank in. If the guy was close, they could be trapped. But as David scrambled to his feet, he felt like he'd woken up groggier than he was before. For the first time, he was glad Rain was taking the lead. He didn't want to add another worry that might slow them down.

Rain had moved their gear toward the entryway and was digging out a path from the cave's mouth into the night. He followed her up the snowbank and into the storm. The cookout ledge was covered in a new layer of snow, and the dents from his skis and rescue sled were barely visible. Was that just yesterday? It felt like much longer since Rain's name had appeared on his phone.

He slipped on his skis, and they moved silently across the cookout ledge and through the narrow passage, back onto the mountain. The snow whipped at his face as he searched for any trace of the man with the gun and his snowmobile. And then he saw it, the same black and silver sled, parked just outside the cave they'd entered. The visibility was low, but David was certain he saw movement. He skied up next to Rain, getting her attention.

"Did you see the snowmobile?"

She nodded.

"I'm not sure I can..." He paused, trying to find a way to say this. "I'm not sure how fast I can go up-hill. I think downhill is our best chance to get away from him."

"But where do we go?"

"We can hope a plow comes this way...or ski all the way into town."

Both of those options were a stretch, but he couldn't think of anything better. Apparently, neither could she, because after a moment, she nodded and turned downhill.

He followed her straight down the mountain, pick-ing up speed, and then they began to weave around the mounds of snow toward stands of trees. David hadn't done this kind of back-country skiing in years, and he hoped the muscle memory would carry him through. He had forgotten this rush, the thrill of ski-ing on a narrow path, staying on his feet, with Rain right in front of him. Despite the wooziness that he hadn't shaken, it felt good.

They were getting some distance, and David told

himself that maybe the guy wouldn't see their tracks. But he could hear the snowmobile's motor now, a low hum from above. Was he heading for them?

Rain pushed with her poles, picking up speed. She looked over her shoulder and saw David following in her tracks. Good. He'd looked a little off since they'd awoken, and she wondered how his arm was holding up. But she hadn't had time to look at it. She zigzagged around snow-covered boulders and dodged trees. They crossed animal tracks enough times to understand they were all headed in the same direction. When she rounded a thick stand of trees, the animal path divided into three branches. Some of the animals had split off in different directions. She knew what that could mean, and it brought her to a stop. David came up behind her.

"Do you think they're hunting?" she asked, her voice quiet.

"Maybe." David was breathing hard, and a dull look in his eyes set her nerves on edge. It didn't matter what was happening up ahead if David collapsed.

"Do you need to rest?"

He shook his head, and she wondered how bad he had to feel before he said yes. She didn't want to find out.

"You have to tell me when to stop," she said, trying to keep her voice practical, trying to smother the emotion that kept welling up in her when she saw his injury.

David's eyes met hers, and he gave a little nod. "I will."

She tried to believe that, but everything she knew about him suggested he'd push through this day, regardless of his own limits.

"I'm going to try to steer around the far right path." She looked out into the blowing snow. "But it'll be hard to tell how close we are."

"I'll follow your lead."

Rain turned, lining up her skis outside the path and trying to steer away from the animals while keeping them pointed downhill. As they descended, dark shadows rose, maybe a story high. She knew this area. The rocks that curved around to split the mountainside were visible from Crystal Ridge. They'd hiked here in the summer. If they had turned off earlier, they would have ended up on the top of the wall, above the animals' path, but it was too late for that. They were cornered here. With a pack of animals. And the only way out was the one straight ahead.

The wind was no longer howling in her ears, and through the gusts came a yip, then another one. Wolves.

David would know what all of this meant as well as she did, so she pushed on, keeping as close to the rock wall, as far from the animal tracks as she could.

But soon, there was no choice. The tracks were in sight again. She and David were heading straight for these animals. Rain told herself that maybe these weren't wolves, and maybe they weren't hunting. But everything around her poked holes in her optimism. The animals were chasing something, and the howls suggested that they had found it.

Before Rain could fully digest what that meant, she heard growls, lower, through the wind. They were getting closer to the wolves, but she still couldn't see them through the blowing snow. How could she steer around them when she couldn't see where they were? The motor of the snowmobile droned in the distance, louder than before.

Panic was welling up inside her, and she had the urge to reach for David. She wanted to feel the comfort of his arms wrapped around her, knowing that whatever they faced, they'd face it together. But they didn't have each other anymore, even if he wouldn't turn away from her. He'd probably hold her, even with the bullet wound burning in his arm...the wound that wouldn't be there if not for her. That thought was enough to stop her cold.

Please Lord, give me the strength to get through this. Give us the presence of mind to figure this out. For David.

Rain searched, deep down inside, for the calm she had found before, for the strength to go on, for the comfort, and for the trust in the path that was in front of her. The spark was still there inside, and she focused on it, fueling it with the very last shred of her hopes. She took a deliberate breath. A second one. The panic eased a little, so she took another long breath, stronger this time. *You are not alone.* Maybe the words were from her father, or maybe they were her own, coming from deep down. Maybe she was stronger than she believed she was. But whosever words these were, at that moment, she chose to believe them.

David knew they were caught. Behind them, the snowmobile's motor ground out its ominous whine, and in front of them, more yips and grunts sounded through the trees. The ridge to their right wasn't high, but it was long and far too steep to get over. It was no wonder the animals were here. The ridge gave shelter from the storm, and it was also a perfect place to trap prey. The only way out was to the left, but that would be a slow journey up the slight incline before they could start down the mountain again. Right now, David needed a rest. He wasn't going to get one.

As he surveyed their surroundings, the wind died down further. Large flakes fell, picked up by sudden gusts and then dropping, floating in front of him. David and Rain were lower on the mountain, below the cloud line, and the veil of the blizzard was lifting. As David strained to look ahead, he saw what he'd known in his gut. Wolves. Maybe twenty feet downhill from them. There were five of them, four adult and one smaller, and they were focused on something in the snow in the middle of them. He caught glimpses of tan and red. A deer, he guessed, judging from the size of the mess. Despite the danger on every front, David couldn't help but marvel at what he was looking at. The wolves' gray pelts were streaked with white, their lean and strong bodies full of energy, despite the heavy snows that made winter hunting difficult. The known packs in California were farther north, but he'd read in the newspaper that a forest camera had caught a few shots of untagged wolves passing by not far from here. When he was called in for a fire in the Tahoe Wilderness last summer, just south of here, he had heard rumors from locals of a wolf sighting. This was a pack, and as far as he could see, they were thriving.

He glanced over at Rain. Worry clouded her face.

"This is probably the only time we'll ever see this," he whispered.

She blinked up at him in surprise, and the full truth of what he'd said hit him. There was a chance they wouldn't make it through the day. And even if they did, the *we* would disappear soon after. They only had those moments.

So far, the wolves hadn't noticed them. But that would change if the wind began to blow from the west instead of from the north. The arm of David's coat was covered with blood, and he was sure that he'd undone some of Rain's efforts to stanch the bleeding. Were wolves attracted to human blood? He wished he'd researched those kinds of details when he first heard the wolf rumors, but he'd have to assume the answer was yes. They really needed to get out of here, yet it was hard to look away from these creatures, both beautiful and brutal.

David glanced at Rain. For a moment, she was as mesmerized as he was. Then she frowned.

"What's our next move?"

David tilted his head to the left, the only direction without danger. "Circle around the wolves and pray the wind doesn't change?"

Praying had been on his mind a lot since he discovered Rain at the bottom of Crystal Ridge on the cookout ledge. Was God still listening, despite all of David's doubts?

Rain glanced to the left. It was a bare stretch, with just gentle rolling hills of white. "Are you sure you can handle the uphill again?"

"I'll make it." How fast he could move at this point was another question.

They had already stood still too long, so Rain turned and headed through the snow. A gust of wind came head-on, followed by another as they skied around the pack. He kept his eyes on the wolves. So far, they hadn't noticed him and Rain. But the snowmobile's motor was no longer background noise. It was getting closer. He looked up the hill and spotted the flash of the man's reflective goggles above a boulder through the snow. The man was a good distance away, but there was no way David and Rain were going to make it around the wolves before the guy got to them. The guy was taking it slowly, zigzagging down, but he was progressing. The blizzard was letting up, so they no longer had the cover of the weather to hide behind. They were exposed.

Still, David pushed ahead, following in Rain's tracks. He glanced up at her, studying the way she bent forward as she forged a path up the hill. Rain was the most determined person he'd ever met, and seeing her fight so hard against the odds filled him with a new burst of hope. Maybe they could make it out of this.

He looked back to check on the wolves, and what he saw sent a chill through him. One of them was no longer looking at the meat in front of it. The wolf was staring straight at him. Was it the sound of the snowmobile or his and Rain's scents that had gotten its attention? Their attacker was getting close. Had he seen the wolves? Maybe he didn't care. Maybe he was banking on his gun and his snowmobile to get him out of this. David wasn't so sure. He'd had enough encounters with animals to know that things could get unpredictable quickly.

Rain was picking up speed, and he took that as a sign that she was just as aware that their position was getting tighter and tighter. One way or another, they were about to get caught. Still, he dug deep into the reserves of his energy and pushed forward, try- ing to use his poles for leverage in the deep snow. When he looked at the pack again, two more wolves had turned around. They stared at him and Rain, their muzzles red with blood and their crouch low and menacing.

The snowmobile's motor dulled to an idle. David whipped around to find the guy had come to a stop on a ledge just behind them, less than ten yards up- hill.

"You're trapped, Rain," said the guy. "Regretting you turned down my offer yet?"

David wondered the same thing. Should he have let her go back before they crossed the summit? Would Rain have been better off that way? But she just ig- nored him and kept skiing.

"We've gotten the wolves' attention," David warned.

"I can take care of that," the assailant retorted.

He pulled his gun out from his jacket and let it dangle by his side. Was he going to shoot the wolves? The thought left a sickening heaviness in David's stomach.

Over his right shoulder, David could see that all the wolves were looking at them. Waiting. The man didn't seem to register the threat. He had the over- confidence that carrying a weapon too often brought.

"I need your help, Rain," said the man. "I'm just the messenger. Your brother screwed over a lot of people, and they're not happy about it. They'll come for you. If it's not me, it'll be someone else. You can't escape this."

For the first time, David could hear that there was fear in his voice, too. This goon was in this just as deeply as Brandon, if not more. That made him even more dangerous. He was never going to give up.

"Just come with me now, and this will be over. I'll leave your friend to fend for himself up here."

Rain was silent as she continued through the snow. Was she considering his offer this time? Maybe she was, or maybe she was just buying them time. Pain was lancing through David's arm, and he wasn't sure how much longer he could keep this up. His legs were less steady than he'd have liked them to be. He'd made it through more arduous days than this one, but the loss of blood was starting to get to him. He gritted his teeth and kept going. The man drove slowly, following them.

"Remember that if you're not going to help me, then you're no good to me alive, Rain," the gunman said. "Then you're a liability."

David's stomach turned at this statement.

"But everyone has a price," said the man, "and I am starting to think yours is wrapped up in this guy right here."

Up ahead of him, Rain's stride faltered. It happened so quickly, just for a moment, and then she pushed on, as strong as before. Had he imagined it? His heart didn't care. The last embers of hope he'd tried so hard to snuff out flamed to life. It was impossible hope, but love never listened to reason. Right here, stranded in the middle of the mountain, David had to face the truth. His love for her still burned, after five years, and it probably never would go away.

They progressed toward the stand of trees ahead.

"I can give your friend better odds," said the guy, and he pointed his gun at the wolf pack.

"No," shouted Rain, but the guy smiled and aimed.

Chapter Eleven

Rain froze, staring at the man, waiting for the gun's explosion. It didn't come, at least not the ear-splitting sound she'd already heard too many times today. Instead, there was a pop. What had just happened? The guy had pulled the trigger, but it hadn't gone off the way it was supposed to. He stared at his gun, and Rain whipped around to find all five wolves looking at them. All unharmed as far as she could tell.

Rain wasn't a gun person, and the only one she had ever fired was the old rifle stored somewhere in the cabin, gathering dust. Her father hadn't been much for guns, either, but he had liked to be in the wilderness enough to recognize the value of hunting, if the need should arise. She had forgotten that rifle even existed until she had heard the pop sound.

It all came back to her. It was summer, and they were out in the forest, with a bull's-eye target pinned to a tree some distance away. Her father had shown her how to steady the rifle against her shoulder, how to widen her stance to brace for the kickback when it fired. He'd made her practice until she was confident enough to do every step on her own, and the next day they'd practiced until she hit the inside circle of the target each time she shot. All along her father had peppered the instructions with warnings, including one about a popping sound. It happened when the bullet didn't have enough push to leave the chamber.

You'll know because the rifle won't kick. And if you fire again without clearing the barrel, the gun can explode.

Was this what happened? Rain looked up to find the man still staring at the gun, his face shifting from surprise to anger. Whatever had happened had rendered his gun unusable. Rain's heart soared as she took in this turn of events and the power shift it meant. If this guy no longer had a working gun, the chances of Rain and David getting out of this alive had increased.

David seemed to know this as well as she did, and he shouted, "Let's go."

Rain took one more look at the wolves, then pushed as hard as she could. The thick flakes fell, thickening the blanket over the forest floor, but without the wind, the visibility was much better, which meant they could go faster. So could the snowmobile.

Rain pushed on, picking up speed. Her legs were shaking with exhaustion, and she was sure David wasn't in any better condition. She had to be careful, not cutting their turn too close to the trees or to the rocks that jutted up haphazardly on the mountain. They were getting lower in elevation, and the pines were getting thicker, blocking their view of what lay just below. But she knew what was downhill. The wolves, waiting for them.

The snowmobile motor gunned. Rain glanced over her shoulder and saw the guy was following in their path again. Anger and setbacks would make a guy like this reckless. She had seen this kind of thing back when she was still working in the emergency room. People came in with everything from concussions to lost fingers, with stories she never wanted to think about again, all from trying to wrest control from a spiraling feeling of loss. If ever there was a candidate for recklessness, this man was it. His comments just minutes ago had suggested that this wasn't just about money for him. More was at stake. The weapons Brandon hid were a threat to him, and probably to the guy's family, too. She and David were still in danger.

David. She caught a glimpse of him as she turned. He wasn't far behind, and she was almost sure his expression was pained. How much blood had he lost? At least he wasn't using his left arm since they were headed downhill.

Rain tried to angle their path farther north, away from the wolf pack, but they were still much too close. As David and Rain passed, all five wolves came into view, watching as they approached. It would take just one of the wolves deciding to pursue them for this chase to be over. Was their instinct to chase her stronger than the urge to stay with the prey they'd already caught?

The snowmobile drew closer, and the incline, steeper. She remembered this part of the hill from the days when they'd make this run when they were teens. The mountain got steeper and rockier, and it would continue like this until David and Rain hit the first switchback of the one road that led from Crystal Lake down to Clover Valley. The trees were dense and thick, so she needed to take it slowly. It was hard to know what might be lurking behind the next turn. She could no longer see the wolves out of the corner of her eyes. Were the animals on their tail, too?

She skied around one thick pine, then another, going as quickly as she could. It didn't matter. Their pursuer on the snowmobile was getting closer. Closer. She was pushing herself as hard as she could, and it wasn't enough. It wouldn't be enough. Despair was setting in as he slowed down behind them. The attacker could keep this up longer than they could.

His words from before came back to her. *Then you're no good to me alive.* She had been hoping to outrun him, to hide and find their way to help, but doubts about her plan were weighing her down. Maybe she should bargain with him instead.

She took another turn around a bushy fir and found herself facing a short, squat boulder, shoulder-height and covered in white. She wedged her skis hard in the snow and turned, just before she hit it. Her legs trembled as she reduced her speed almost to a stop, and Rain drew in a sharp breath.

David was right behind her. If she didn't move, he'd crash into her. Quickly, she pushed ahead.

"Watch the turn," she called back to David, praying he could hear it over the gunning of the snowmobile's motor.

She pushed again with her poles, getting out of the way just as David crashed around the tree, coming straight for the boulder.

"Turn," she yelled.

He turned, skidding to a stop. Her heart jumped in her chest at how close he'd just come to disaster.

"Keep going," he growled.

The motor revved so close behind, as she scrambled ahead, trying to get out of the way before the snowmobile came around the corner. She couldn't move her arms and legs fast enough, and she forced herself not to look back. This was it. If she didn't move faster, David couldn't get out of the way. And this man would hit David.

Please, God, David brings so much good to the world. He dedicates his life to protecting people. Please keep him safe.

The snowmobile motor revved again, and then

there was a crunch of metal hitting rock. The motor screeched, and Rain's stomach dropped out as she came to a stop. There was a grunt, and over the boulder she caught a glimpse of reflective goggles as their attacker was launched into the deep snow. Rain was frozen in place. The whole sequence had lasted two seconds, maybe three, but those moments left her suspended in time as panic and dread filled her, threatening to drown her.

If David hadn't survived…

But his ski tip peeked out from behind the boulder, then his poles. Then David himself. He wasn't hit.

Time began again. David skied down next to her and stopped, and something far more than relief ran through her. It ran too deep, too strong, threatening to crumble the wall she'd built these last five years. She pushed that feeling aside.

"What happened to…?"

The nurse in her needed to scramble back up the hill, but the fear she'd experienced these last two days held her in place. This was a terrible man, a weapons trafficker, yet, when she was in the emergency room, she didn't ask questions before she helped people who came through those doors. Could she leave someone out here, dying in the forest?

She thought back to that woman and baby in the trailer. Was this man the father? Rain knew what it was to lose a parent, however imperfect they were.

She didn't know for sure what these relationships were, but if he was the father, and he had a baby... the baby didn't ask for any of this. She couldn't let go of this idea. She wouldn't wish the death of a parent on anyone, no matter who that parent was. *Even if that parent had killed her brother?* With that thought came the injustice of it, of her brother's death, of being left alone in the world. Her brother had been involved in bad things, but he was her last connection to her family. He deserved consequences, but not death. Shouldn't she extend the same grace to that baby in the trailer?

Their attacker was moving, shifting in the snow. He yelled out a profanity, and it was all she needed to let go of her drive to help. She glanced at David. He was doubled over, resting one arm on his thigh. If she didn't get him help, he was the one who was going to die. That was the priority.

"You need to rest more?" she asked David.

"Let's get some distance from this guy."

The fear welled up again, a sharp echo of the panic she'd felt moments ago.

Rain skied down, weaving a path in the snow, leaving the man behind. She caught glimpses of the road, a snakelike plane of white breaking up the forest below, and her heart beat faster. Once they hit the road, they could rest.

The last stretch was bare, the trees cleared from the mountainside next to the road and the snow piled high up the sides. She started down the last bank at an angle, then came to a stop on the untouched blanket of snow. There was so much relief when she turned around to see David following behind. But that relief turned to fear as she watched his legs collapse under him. He tumbled down, breaking his fall at the edge of the road.

David was back in his bedroom, which was also somehow the hospital. It was after that big fire... except it was cold, really cold. Rain was there, too. And he knew what was coming. He remembered her words perfectly as she spoke them again.

This hurts too much. I can't handle a life like this, watching you take these risks.

It hurt just as much as it had the last time. When he tried to respond, no sound came. He couldn't do better this time. He couldn't tell her he was less reckless now, that he understood why she was so worried. The pain was still there. Not just the physical pain but the heartache of loss. He knew what to say this time, but his voice didn't work...

"David?" Her voice came again.

David blinked, the space between dreams and waking dissolving. He wasn't in his bedroom, and he wasn't in a hospital. He was out on the mountain, and Rain was looking down at him with a mixture of fear and... It hurt to even think about what else that could be. He hadn't had this dream about his last day with Rain in a long time. The events of the day must be messing with his head. But as he looked up at her, memories and dreams blurred together, a cacophony of years of dissonances all coming into tune and playing in the same key. He was in love with Rain. She peered down at him, those beautiful brown eyes filled with a softness, a tenderness. A closeness. She reached for him, brushing snow out of his hair, off his face, and the connection between them grew stronger.

Everything was coming back. The call. The rescue sled. The shattering of glass when the man shot through the window. The caves. The wolves. The snowmobile crash. He had dreamed that hospital scene. In reality, he and Rain were on the side of the road, miles away from everything. Still in danger.

He blinked up at her, trying to contain the surge of emotions stirring inside him. "How long have I been out?"

"Long enough to tumble down that snowbank." Her words were quick, but her voice wavered. "Do you remember what happened?"

David traced his memory of the chase, the crunch of metal on rock as a snowmobile hit it, and the man with a gun.

He was lying down with his legs propped up on his backpack. David scrambled to sit up, but stars clouded his vision as soon as he was upright. He swayed, then caught himself with his good arm, his poles dangling from his wrists.

"Whoa, slow down," said Rain, pressing his good shoulder.

"But the man—"

She shook her head. "There's no sign of him yet. It'll take a while for him to get this far. And he no longer has a working gun. Do you remember that?"

Yes, he remembered. He also noticed she'd taken off her skis and that she was kneeling next to him, which suggested he'd been out for at least a couple minutes.

"We need to move soon," he said, shifting his weight, testing his strength. It was far from ideal. David's arm hurt more and more. He was sure that wasn't a good sign. "Even if that man is moving slowly, we don't know where the wolves are."

"We'll go, but you've lost enough blood to make you pass out," said Rain. "I need to take a look at your arm."

David frowned as a chill ran through his body. He'd started to cool down, all the way to his core. "I really need to move, to warm up."

She shook her head. "I can't let you get up. Not yet."

Her gaze was intense, and her mouth was set in a determined line. His heartbeat surged. She was so beautiful like this, and he wanted to argue with her, just to come up against her will of steel one more time. But he didn't have the energy. Or maybe it was something else.

She searched through her pack and pulled out gauze, a Swiss army knife, a plastic bag and the duct tape. She laid them on her pack, using it as an impromptu hospital tray. David shivered.

"I was hoping I wouldn't have to do this, but you're losing too much blood. I need to get a look at this wound again," she said. "But that means we're going to need to take this arm out of your coat."

Just the thought of it was making him cold, but he didn't have much choice. He trusted her, at least in this area. But he wasn't sure how far. She took out her Swiss army knife. He eyed it warily as she started clipping away at the duct tape that patched his jacket together. Then she unwrapped the bandanna from around his arm. Blood pumped through his arm, setting off the sensation of pins and needles in his hand, and he winced.

She must have seen his reaction, because she frowned. "I'll go as quickly as I can. But I'm going to need you to turn away."

"I can handle it. I'd rather know how bad this is," he said, shaking his head.

Rain gave him a pointed look. "I know you're tough and can handle anything."

He thought he detected a hint of sarcasm, but it was gone when she spoke again.

"It's for me. I need to forget this is you. Because I

can't treat someone I…" She swallowed. "Someone I know."

David's insides twisted as he heard that last word. He was just someone she knew. Why had he been hoping she'd say something more? He nodded and looked away as she eased the jacket off his left shoulder.

"Just tell me if you think you're going to pass out again," she added.

"I'll try my best." He was going for the same wry tone he could have used with *people he knew*, but David couldn't help thinking that this didn't bode well for what was coming next. Still, he was not going to slow them down any more.

This made him want to see her face even more right now, just to see how bad she thought it was, but this was her work. He needed to respect that.

The cold air blew inside his jacket against his layers, and he tried not to shiver as she snipped his shirt, stripping away a part of it. The first snowflakes fell on his bare skin, and he gritted his teeth as the cold wind lashed his arm. She twisted off the cap of the water bottle, and the cold, wet water hit his arm.

"These first aid kits have a hundred little plastic bandages and no syringe for irrigating wounds," she muttered as another splash of water hit his arm.

Then there was something soft—gauze, he guessed—and the stinging feeling got stronger, every moment stretching infinitely long as pain lanced through him. The icy cold of the night air kept him sharp, even through the worst of it. Then the prodding and wiping was over, and he heard the duct tape stretching off its roll. She wrapped it around his arm. He breathed a sigh of relief. The worst of it was over, at least for now. Plastic crumpled, from his bandages, most likely, and then she taped his jacket together again.

"Can I turn back now?" he asked.

"Yes," she said, but her voice was shaky. Her hands were bare and pink, and he wanted to warm them with his.

"How bad is it?"

He watched her face carefully, the dart of her gaze, the way her mouth turned down at the corners into a little frown. "The good news is that you made it this far. The bad news is that the wound is continuing to bleed, and I don't know if the bullet nicked your bone on the way through. The bandaging worked, but you've lost a lot of blood, and I'm not sure…"

She didn't have to finish that sentence. There was a whole list of uncertainties running through his mind. Like the fact that they were in the middle of the Tahoe National Wilderness, it was night, the snow still hadn't let up, and he wasn't even sure he could stand up at this point. Those were only the immediate dangers that occurred to him.

But a deeper uncertainty had set in, too. The pain from his arm was making him vulnerable to the emotions that he'd worked so hard to keep out, and as she looked at him, those wounds felt raw, exposed. He had felt this way before, when her parents had died, and he had felt it again when he had woken up in the hospital room after that fire to find her in the chair next to him. It was that look on her face, the look of pain, in danger of overwhelming her, breaking her. Watching her brought back that helplessness that had pulled him down. He wanted to fix it, do something to help her. In the end he couldn't do anything about it. But as she stared down at him, frustration ran through him. He would not let his body give up on him. He would not cause Rain any more pain. *Please, God. This is for her.*

"What's your name?"

"David Hernandez."

Her eyes softened.

"Where are we?"

"On the road to Clover Valley."

She bit her lip. Swallowed.

"What year is it?"

"Five years since we've been together."

She didn't look away, and neither did he. The snow was falling everywhere, landing on her hat, glistening in her hair, melting on her cheeks. For one quiet moment, he let himself feel how much he'd missed her. How much he wished they were still together.

"Are you queasy?" she asked, breaking the spell.

He shook his head. "Just exhausted."

Rain pulled out her phone, and David felt a little glimmer of hope. If she found a signal, she could call for help. But that glimmer of hope died quickly when she frowned.

"Nothing. We need to head down the mountain."

David was trying to combat the fear and darkness that was creeping into his thoughts. Why would God have chosen this path for them? But this path had brought them back together, too. And as he looked at her, he felt the blessing of it, even if it was temporary.

Rain stowed her phone.

"We need to find a way to get you to Clover Valley, to the urgent care." She paused. "And hope someone is there in this storm."

Chapter Twelve

Rain was trying to hide her fear from David, and she was doing a terrible job at it. But she had to find a way to stay levelheaded, to block out the emotions and focus on the next steps.

Back when she worked in the emergency room, she had been so much better at remaining composed. Was she so far out of practice, or were her hands shaking because of the person in front of her? She'd made David turn away, hoping it would help her block out the overwhelming dread running through her body, but it wasn't working. Pain, longing, distress—all these long-buried emotions were leaking in. The walls she had erected for years were crumbling, walls she desperately needed to keep out the connection to him, and she had to do something to prop them back up.

She concentrated on each detail, but each detail was connected to David. She helped him slide the strap of his pack over his arm, trying not to disturb his wound, and that focus worked for a moment, but when he shifted, she caught a glimpse of his profile. The angle of his jawline, the warm brown of his eye so close, so familiar. When she helped him stand, the first moments were filled with unease that he might collapse again. She could focus on the immediate, the practical. But when he straightened and smiled, his expression hit her deep inside. He used to smile at her like that all the time. Even dusting off her own skis brought back a flood of memories of all those times they had gone out on ski trips together. By the time she started downhill, the feeling that she had tried so hard to resist wouldn't stay contained any longer. She still loved this man. Another thought followed, one even more paralyzing than the last. It was one that had shaken her five years ago and still did today. This love for David had a power to destroy her. Rain had suffered so much loss, and she could think of too many ways that this day could go wrong. Blood loss, hypothermia, wolves, the man still bent on finding them... Fear was overtaking her. Years ago, she would've turned to David for support, but she had no right to do that now. She was alone, drowning in her fear. She had no one left.

You have God.

The words came from somewhere inside, strong and clear. She answered them in a prayer.

Let David live. Even if we're not meant to be to-

gether, I need him to be alive in this world. Not just for me. I don't want his family to suffer his loss. Please.

Rain took a long breath as the fear eased its stranglehold on her. She took another, and another, and when she no longer was paralyzed, she looked up. David's gaze was on her, his brow creased with concern.

"Are you okay?" he asked. "Is it your ankle?"

"My ankle is fine." Her voice sounded much more level than she felt, for which she was grateful. "Should we take the road, or can you handle the forest?"

The road was flat, easy skiing, but it zigzagged in a series of switchbacks down the mountain. It was the long route. The forest was more direct, but it took more maneuvering, which might require more energy than David had. He glanced up at the mountain. There were enough rustles for her to think the man was following their path down. They really needed to keep moving.

"Forest," he said. "At least for now."

He was looking a little less pale, and she told herself this was a good sign.

"We'll give it a try. But this time, let me know when you need a break before you pass out."

David's lips held a hint of a smile, one that gave her a smidgen of hope. "I'll do my best."

They started up the embankment that plows had created after earlier snows, and then they glided down into the woods. The snowfall was tapering off, the big flakes fluttering down gradually as she forged a trail through the deep powder. She slowed in a clearing to check on David, who was much steadier than she would have been if she had been shot in the arm. She continued around trees and over unidentifiable obstacles covered in white. The forest was dense here, so it was hard to see at a distance, but they made it to another embankment, marking the next switchback in the road. She skied down the plow's hill and stopped on the road, with its new, thick layer of untouched snow, then turned back to wait for David. He was right behind her, and this time he was still on his feet.

"Let's take another break," she said, then sat down in the snow before he could answer.

At this point, she knew better than to ask him if he needed it. He'd always seemed to see himself as invulnerable, and this really wasn't the time to take up that argument.

"Anything changed since before the last time we stopped?" She tried to make the question sound casual.

"I didn't pass out this time," he said with a hint of a smile.

"I noticed." His eyes were soft, serious but warm. It was impossible to ignore how good it felt to sit here, in the quiet of the newly fallen snow. No matter what was coming, this moment existed for them. The thought triggered a burst of warmth deep inside.

She was grateful for this moment, even if they were far from out of danger.

"We're putting some distance between us and that guy," she said. "But what do we do about him? If a plow comes by, they'll pick him up, and as soon as the roads are clear, he'll escape."

Rain took out her phone and checked the screen. "Still no reception, and my battery is low now."

She frowned and turned it off. They needed to get moving again. She looked at David, taking in his pale cheeks and drooping eyelids. The fact that he was still upright and talking was impressive. As far as she could tell, he was managing. But Clover Valley was miles away, and she had no idea how far they'd have to travel to get cell service.

"Are you happy?" David asked.

She blinked, thrown off by the question. What should she say? She loved her job and she had friends and her church. Did that outweigh the loneliness that had grown through the years? Maybe if she had been prepared for it, she might have answered more carefully. But the truth came out before she could think better of it.

"I don't know how to answer that," she said. "I'm not unhappy."

David tilted his head a little, studying her. "Not the same thing."

Oh, how well she knew that. "Are you?"

"In some ways."

She wondered which ways. Did he have a girlfriend? Probably. He had never had trouble attracting attention, even when he did nothing to encourage it. Brave, strong, caring… Actually, she didn't want to think about that.

"I read about that fire just south of here that happened last summer, the one that was headed for South Lake Tahoe," she said. "I wondered if you were there."

He looked at her with mild surprise, as if he hadn't expected her to bring up the wedge between them. "We got lucky on that one. The flames had jumped the fire line, but then the wind switched directions long enough that we got it under control."

"Were you close to the fire?" Did she even want to know? Yes, it was better this way.

"Not too close," he said.

Rain wasn't so sure they had the same definition of too close.

"In some ways, forest fires can be safer for firefighters than the ones we get called to in Sacramento, at least the jobs I was doing," he said. "It's a lot of digging, making fire lines and evacuating residents," he added. "Jobs like hotshots, the people who drop down into the middle—they are the ones who take the biggest risks."

But he was still on the Cal fire team. If they were together, she'd watch him leave every summer to fight the fires that swept through California. But God had taken care of him for these five years. Maybe that was enough.

* * *

David wasn't going to make it. He knew his body's limits after years of testing them, and he was getting closer to them. But there was no other choice except to grit his teeth and push forward.

Skiing the road was easier, the gentle glide requiring less effort. If he just focused on keeping himself standing, he could hold out for a while. But each turn, each time he sank down, stars clouded his vision. The pain in his arm was not getting any better, either. But none of that was his biggest concern. His greatest fear right now was that if he passed out, Rain wouldn't leave him. She would stay with him, even if it meant she would freeze out here. He had to find a way to talk to her about this, to convince her that if he couldn't make it, she needed to continue alone. But how? It was against her nature to leave someone who needed help. And he couldn't fault her for that. This had always been something they had in common.

David followed Rain's trail, pushing up against his exhaustion until he couldn't take it any longer.

"I need to rest," he said. The words barely came out, but the night was quiet enough for her to hear them. She skied to the side of the road and sat down, and it was all he could do not to collapse again. He didn't want to scare her. Rain sized him up, concern written in the crease between her eyes and the gentle frown playing at her lips. He still hadn't found a good way to tell her to go ahead without him, so he just went straight for it.

"I don't think I can make it much farther," he said. "I think it's best if you go ahead and find help, not wait until I pass out."

Her eyes widened. "You know I can't do that, David."

"It's my best chance," he said, his voice low. "You know it. You know that's the logical choice."

Tears were welling in her eyes, and she shook her head. "Nothing about this makes any sense. Even if the storm has let up enough that I find a signal, I don't think you'll make it out here for that long." At those last words, her voice wavered.

It hurt to see her emotion leaking through. There had been years when he would have grabbed on to these shreds of evidence that she still cared about him, but there was no joy in seeing her upset like this.

"You can ski into town. The weather is clearing up. You can try 911, or you can try my sister's phone," he said. "She'd come with our snowmobile."

Rain turned to look down the empty road, the untouched snow glowing in the night. Then she turned back to him, her mouth in a frown.

"My phone is almost dead."

"Take mine. It's in my pack." He went to reach for it. Even that much movement was pushing him to the edge of consciousness.

Rain struggled through the snow, climbing around to get it for him.

"In the front pocket," he added.

The drag of the zipper rang through the quiet of the night. "We can trade. If you somehow get service, I'll figure out a way to get to you."

She stowed his phone in her own pack, then found the pen. She raised his sleeve to expose his bare skin, then wrote down a number.

"Here's the passcode to unlock mine." She lifted up her own sleeve and looked at him expectantly. "What's yours?"

Flakes of snow fell on her skin, turning to tiny drops of water as she waited for his answer. His brain was definitely not fully functioning, because he hadn't seen this problem coming. He swallowed and looked straight at her. "It's your birthday. Year, month, then day. I never bothered to change it."

It hurt to confess this. He had forgotten that the passcode was connected to her, or at least that was what he told himself. But deep down he knew better. He'd held on to this last scrap of their time together, and he'd shown it to her, exposed the part of him that he never wanted her to see. She closed her eyes, and her mouth trembled a little, but she said nothing, just nodded and stuffed the pen back into her pack.

She pulled out a reflective blanket and unfolded it, then laid it on the ground, next to the snowbank. David sat down on it. He unbuckled his pack and slid off one arm, and she knelt next to him to help him with the other. Good news: he didn't black out. She wrapped the blanket around him as well as she could.

Even now, he couldn't stop thinking about her eyes. Deep brown and filled with compassion. How he had ached for this chance to be here again, to see her, to connect like this with Rain. How he had prayed for it. His prayers were being answered, but not at all in the way he had hoped. She was about to leave him on the side of the road in the middle of the winter. His sweat from exertion on the mountain was cooling much too quickly. He wasn't sure how long it would be until he started shivering. But he put aside these worries and focused on her eyes, finding solace in them.

"This is what I was afraid of the whole time. Five years ago I left you so this would never happen. I never wanted to feel so scared again. How can we be back here?" Her voice wavered on that last question.

David knew she wasn't just talking to him. She was talking to God, too. And that moment, every bit of her sorrow ran through him. He wasn't even mad anymore that she had left, not when he could hear how hard it had been for her.

Could they ever be together again? Earlier today he'd said his job meant that he'd never consider a family, but everything was different with Rain... No. He couldn't let that thought in. She'd left him before, and no matter how good it felt to be with her right now, nothing had changed. He'd never be able to trust that she could handle the danger he was in, and he wasn't sure he could handle leaving her every day, knowing he might not return. But the warmth of her nearness was too much to resist.

She put her hands over her heart, and a rush of happiness ran through him. Then she leaned closer until her jacket brushed against his. She paused, and her eyes closed just an inch from him, as if she, too, were savoring their closeness. He leaned forward, closing that last distance once again, and kissed her. Soft, warm comfort ran through him. *You are not alone.*

He loved her. The thought hit him hard, but he had the sense not to let those words slip from his mouth. He wouldn't let himself get hurt like that again. So he said, "I'll be okay here. Just try to get in touch with my sister. And then come back for me."

Even that last sentence felt so heavy, so loaded with their past. She didn't say anything as she stood up, and she didn't look back as she skied away. And despite all the warning bells going off in his head, as he watched her, he found himself praying.

Thank You, God, for giving me this moment. Thank You for bringing us here.

Chapter Thirteen

Rain didn't let herself look back. She pushed ahead, one ski, then the other, numbing herself to the exhaustion that ran through her legs with each stride. She was leaving David behind when his body had given up on him. When he needed her the most.

But she needed him, too. She was still in love with him.

Logic told her that David was right that she had to go for help alone, but everything about this echoed of their past. She was no longer working by logic. She was leaving him to bleed out by the roadside. In the cold. With an attacker following him.

After all, she was the one who had gotten him into this. That thought drove her forward. She could not let him die out here.

Come back for me. His words resonated through her body.

Rain skied down the snowbank and into the forest,

ignoring the burn in her legs. When she got to the next switchback, she pulled David's phone out of her pocket and turned it on. She tried to ignore the pain of typing out his pass code, but it was everywhere. There were no more walls to keep this mixture of hurt and the hope it brought. But with that hope came the threat of loss, too. A loss she couldn't handle.

No signal yet. She shoved the phone into her pocket again and made her way to the forest. Only a few more switchbacks, and then she'd hit the river. After that, the road followed the water, curving next to it into town. By then, she definitely would have a signal, but it would take at least an hour to get there. David didn't have an hour, probably not with the man on their tail and definitely not in the cold. She sped over the next embankment and the next, each time checking the phone. She was panting, her heart racing as she doubled over, trying to catch her breath. She pulled the device out and stared at the screen. One little bar appeared. Did that mean the cell towers were working again?

Quickly, she scrolled through David's contacts and found his sister's number. Isabel answered on the first ring.

"David? Are you okay?" Isabel's voice was filled with worry. Rain had been so focused on leaving David behind that she hadn't readied herself for how hard this conversation would be. Isabel's familiar voice came through the line, reminding her of more layers of unresolved hurt she'd tried to leave behind. Tried and failed.

"This is Rain," she said, pushing herself to focus on the mountain of problems in front of them. "David's been shot, and we have to get him to an urgent care facility. I need you to get on your snowmobile and follow the road down to Clover Valley. You'll find him." She bit her lip and added, "Please."

"You're not with him?"

The accusation in her voice stung Rain.

"I had to head down the mountain to find a signal, and I was ready to ski into town for help if I needed to," she said.

"I'll be there as soon as I can." Isabel disconnected the line.

Too late, Rain thought of the man who was pursuing them. He no longer had a gun, but he was still dangerous. She tried to call back Isabel, but there was no signal, so she tried it as a text message. She waited, staring at the screen, until it finally went through. Now she had to pray that Isabel saw it.

Rain then turned around and started back up the hill. It was easier to take the road. Her legs burned and exhaustion threatened to overtake her, but she wouldn't let herself stop. As her skis threaded the snow, her mind raced through all the scenarios she could think about with David and what she should do. Should she have laid him down and put up his feet? And if the wolves had made their way down the mountain to find him…well, she didn't know what she would do.

Rain rounded the last curve, and David came into sight. He was alone, his skis off, and he was leaning against the snowbank. She skied faster until she was right in front of him. His eyes were closed, and his face was pale. Rain knelt down in front of him.

"David?" She didn't even try to hide her panic.

His eyes fluttered open, his dark lashes dotted with snow. "Just resting."

He managed to sound soothing, even in this state, almost as if she were the one brushing up with death. Though maybe that wasn't too far off. If she lost him, it would be a different kind of death, one inside.

"I got a hold of your sister. She's coming."

"Thank you."

At her house, he had thrown accusations about the past at her, but there was no resentment in his voice tonight. The past wasn't hanging between them, and neither was the future. This time she didn't resist the warmth that flooded through her.

David gave her a weak smile. "You made it back."

She wanted to reassure him, to say, *I'll be here for you*, but she couldn't find the right words. She hadn't been there for him, not the last time. How she wished she could change the past.

David had made it. He'd kept himself awake, fought off the heavy fog of sleep that lured him in.

He wouldn't pass out, not when there were things he'd left unsaid between Rain and him.

She was quiet as she sat down next to him, settling herself close. She looked at him, her eyes full of worry while she assessed him. David tried to hide a shiver from her, but he was sure she caught it.

"How are you holding up?" Rain bit her lip as she gazed down at him.

"All right. Trying to stay awake." They both knew that falling asleep would not be a good thing. "I'm thirsty."

"I can give you a sip of water, just to wet your mouth. You shouldn't have anything in your stomach when you get to the urgent care center."

She took out the water bottle and unscrewed the top. He ignored the urge to drink and just poured a little on his tongue, then passed the bottle back to her. It occurred to him that this might be the last time he'd have to sit and talk with her. If he made it through this, they would go their separate ways. So he thought of all the questions he had wondered over the years, when her name came up in passing or when he drove by her cabin on the way to his family's place. He wasn't sure he wanted to know all the answers, but if this was the last chance he had to ask them, his future self would probably regret not trying.

"I'm so sorry about your brother," he said.

She looked at him in surprise. Then she nodded.

"Thank you. It's going to sound a little strange, but as awful as all of this has been yesterday and today, it's a relief, to know all this about him. All his secretive behavior makes sense. I knew that my brother never would accidentally have fallen from Crystal Ridge. It's terrible knowing that he was involved with weapons, but sadly, it's not a complete surprise. I can see how Brandon might have gotten into this. And somehow, that's better than the feeling that's followed me since his death…like I didn't know him in the end." She frowned. "That probably sounds strange coming from someone who has dedicated herself to saving lives. But that's what I'm feeling right now."

He watched her as she spoke, watched the sadness and the loss leak into her expression and her voice. He wished he had been there for her when Brandon died, been there to listen. Even if they hadn't been together, he could have comforted her.

They sat there quietly for a while as he took in her story, thinking about her grief. He wanted so much to imagine that she had some solace somewhere.

The sound of a snowmobile filtered down the mountain. Was it Isabel on her way? If it was, he only needed to hang on for a little longer.

"Rain?"

"Yes?"

"What do you want from the future?"

She swallowed and looked away. "I like my position in the eye clinic. It has regular hours and isn't too stressful, and I feel like I'm bringing something good into the world. But…" She paused, brushing some snow off her pants. "Sometimes I think I want to go back to the ER."

She glanced up at him quickly and added, "I like my apartment, and I've managed to save enough to maybe put a down payment on a house. My church has been really supportive, and I'm grateful for that." She smiled in a way that didn't reach her eyes. "So I guess I'm content."

The sentence came out cheerfully, and he wondered if it was just his imagination or if she really did sound overly cheerful. The desire for her to be all right, to be happy in the world, warred with the selfish want to hear that her life was still missing something. That her life was still missing him. But, as always, the former won. Even if he couldn't have her, knowing she was somewhere out there, happy in the world, was better.

"Are you together with anyone?" he asked.

She shook her head, then frowned. "You?"

"You know my phone's passcode," he said, trying to quirk his lips. She didn't smile back, so he added, "Five years ago, I thought this was the end of our path. Now God has brought us back together. Even if it's just for today, I'm grateful for it. We don't know what our path looks like in the future, Rain. We don't know what God has planned for us, but we still have this moment right now."

Tears were brimming in her eyes, and one spilled over. She brushed it away with her glove. "I love you, David. Still, after all these years, that feeling hasn't gone away."

How he had longed to hear those words. Maybe they were true, and maybe she was just comforting him. The familiar bells clanged out a warning in his head. Even if they were true, love hadn't been enough to keep them together five years ago.

"It's okay. You don't have to say that. Just…" He swallowed. "Just please don't leave yet. If I make it to the hospital in time, just please be there when I wake up."

She opened her mouth to protest, then closed it. Nodded. He could see the tears welling in her eyes, but he didn't want to spend their time on sadness, so he said, "Tell me more about the eye clinic."

As Rain began to tell him about her daily routine and the kinds of patients she saw, he listened, imagining her life, imagining her happy in it. And even as his vision got fuzzier and he felt himself fading out, her voice stayed up with him and followed him into sleep, a reminder of what the best of the world could be.

Chapter Fourteen

"David?" Rain shook his good arm, but he didn't respond. A new wave of fear surged in her as she tried again. "David?"

She scrambled closer and shook him harder. He mumbled something she couldn't make out, but that was better than nothing.

"Wake up, David. Stay with me."

Nothing this time. The snowmobile was getting closer, that ominous sound that had dogged them these last two days. Rain had to remind herself that this time, it meant help. But new problems were cropping up: How could they get him down the mountain if he was passed out? How could they even get him onto the snowmobile?

"Talk to me," she said. "Argue with me. Get mad at me. Anything you want." How they had fought before she'd left, each shooting direct arrows at each other, causing wounds that wouldn't heal. She'd gladly take more of those wounds if they meant he'd live.

The sled remained out of sight, the motor dulled, and it lowered to an idle as another fear occurred to her. Had Isabel missed the message about the attacker? He probably had made his way to the road, and she could have stopped to pick him up.

Please, God, guide her path.

The motor sped up, and she waited, frozen, for the snowmobile to appear. But as she looked up the road, movement from up the mountain caught her eye. The guy with the reflective goggles was running in the snow. He no longer had a gun, but he was coming in quickly, headed straight for her. Rain was on her own to protect both David and herself. Since her parents' death, she'd done everything to avoid the feeling of isolation. That fear had steered her life, pushing her to change jobs and to break up with David. She didn't want to face difficulty alone. But if she turned and skied away now, she'd be leaving David behind, unconscious and helpless. That wasn't an option. The only option was to stay and fight a man larger than her and bent on doing harm.

She looked at her hands, at the ski pole she clung to, as determination filled her.

"I'm not letting you get away," he called down to her. "I'm not letting you ruin this for me."

She didn't waste her time with a response. Instead, she calculated her defense. There had been a few moments in the ER when she'd had to go on the defensive. The best plan was to keep him at a distance and pretend to negotiate with him. But if he came for her... Rain clicked off the bindings of her skis and moved away from David. She prayed she could keep the man focused on her.

He ran down the snowbank, and then he was right in front of her. The man was panting, and he looked just as tired as she felt. He took off his goggles, and a wild recklessness shone in his eyes. This man was desperate.

"I know where my brother hid the guns," she said.

"Do you?" he asked. "You want me to believe you, when I have you cornered?"

He doesn't have you cornered. You're strong and knowledgeable enough to outwit him on the mountain. She could probably outrun this guy on foot, lead him away from David, and she had her poles to defend herself. Her mind calmed, the way it always had in the ER, and she focused on how to get out of this situation.

"I can tell you what's inside of the boxes," she said, stepping backward. The man didn't answer, so she described the gun she'd seen in as much detail as she remembered.

"And you think I believe you'll lead me to them?"

He lunged at her. But Rain was ready. She moved aside and lifted one ski pole to his chest. Using her weight, she shoved him to the side with it. He grabbed the pole in his glove, so she did the same with her other one, shoving again, and he toppled over into the snow, taking one of her poles with him. Rain scrambled to turn and move out of reach. She wasn't sure how long she could keep this up, but if she could continue to move him away from David...

Rain glanced up, and what she saw made her heart leap. A different snowmobile came around the bend, pulling a rescue sled, and she could make out a blue jacket and long, brown hair flowing out from the helmet. Was it Isabel? It had to be, and Rain needed to warn her.

She said a quick thank-you to God, but that hope turned to dread as the man scrambled to stand up again. Was he going to get control of the snowmobile? Rain wouldn't let that happen. She threw herself on top of the man, keeping him facedown and off his feet as the snowmobile came to a stop. The attacker in the deep snow struggled, trying to buck her off...

"Help me," Rain yelled, and Isabel jumped into action. She ran toward the man's feet, pulled them out from under him and kneeled on them. He twisted, grabbing Rain's jacket.

"The tape. In my pack," she panted, trying to hold him off with the tube of her pole. Isabel unzipped her bag, and Rain heard the rip of duct tape. The man yelled and kicked and swore, but Isabel managed to get the duct tape around his feet. Then she inched forward, and so did Rain until they were both sitting on the guy's back, pinning him to the ground. Isabel pulled out more duct tape and taped one hand to his jacket, then the other. The man continued to hurl insults, so Isabel held the duct tape in front of his mouth.

"Your choice," she said.

He quieted immediately.

"You should roll yourself over to the side of the road," said Rain. "We'll send someone for you soon."

Then she turned to Isabel. Rain had a burst of nervousness, wondering what Isabel thought about the mess she'd gotten David into, but she pushed that thought out of her head. They could worry about that later. Right now, they needed to save David's life. That thought put her in nurse mode.

"He passed out just a couple minutes ago. We have to hurry."

Isabel nodded. The road had been plowed after the first snows of the season, so it wasn't nearly as deep as the forest, but the blizzard had dumped a few feet. Isabel moved the snowmobile so the rescue sled was lined up with where her brother was lying, and Rain followed, wading through the knee-high powder toward David, ignoring the grunts from her attacker.

"He's passed out, so we both need to lift him," she said, then added, "But he might wake up from the pain in his arm."

For once, the pain might help them today, though the thought of being the cause of it was like a punch in the gut. *I can't treat someone I love.* She hadn't finished the sentence, and she wondered if he'd understood it anyway.

Rain unbuckled David's pack and eased it off his shoulders. Isabel turned him to one side as she slipped it off one arm, then the other. She positioned herself on the injured side of him, and Isabel stood on the other.

"Ready?" Rain slipped an arm between his shoulder and the backpack, and Isabel did the same. "One, two, three…"

They half lifted, half dragged him onto the orange sled. David mumbled a few words and grabbed for his left arm.

"Your sister is here, David," she said, moving his hand away. "We're getting you help."

His head tipped forward, his eyes closing. David muttered something that she didn't catch.

"What did you say?" Isabel's voice shook.

"Don't leave me, Rain," he whispered.

The words hurt, physically hurt, enough to make her stumble again in the deep snow.

"I won't leave you." She couldn't stop the words from spilling out. She told herself that he just meant until he woke up, like the last time, but it didn't help. She couldn't bear the idea of leaving him. She could feel the old ribbons that bound them together pulling inside, tying themselves again, the ones she had worked so hard to untangle. Rain was starting to realize that she no longer had a choice to resist. Maybe she'd never had one.

"I'm just going to secure the buckles on the sled," she said, but David didn't respond. "David?" Her voice was full of the fear she had tried so hard to rein in.

"Don't worry, Rain," he whispered.

Hearing those words from him as he teetered into unconsciousness almost broke her. He'd use his last words to comfort her. Isabel climbed onto the snowmobile.

"I'll be right behind you," Rain said. "David's going to make it."

She said it with more confidence than she felt. Isabel's lips trembled as she nodded. She started the motor and drove away into the night.

Rain watched them disappear around the curve, leaving her alone. It was only then that she began to shiver. Her legs crumpled underneath her, and her arms shook. Her fingers fumbled with the poles as the fear flooded in, the fear she'd tried to keep at bay.

Though she had learned how to set her emotions aside, waiting until the crisis was over before letting those feelings in, they had to come in sometime. Now that David was gone, now that his fate was out of her hands, the fear crashed in.

Every dream that had haunted her, every night she'd stayed up, waiting to hear from him—each one of these memories came to life. He might not make it. The tears that she'd fought flowed freely now, and she sobbed into the quiet night, loss and mourning covering her.

Rain wasn't sure how long she sat there, but the cold began to creep in, reminding her that this day was far from over. Her pursuer had moved himself to the side of the road. Rain took out her phone and took a few pictures of him. When he opened his mouth to protest, she held out the tape again. He chose to stay silent, and she left him there, clicked on her skis and headed toward town.

The night was quiet, the snow still falling. Remorse was sneaky, wily, creeping up at the lowest of times. This day had left her vulnerable, and now, as she skied into the cold night air, she couldn't fight back her emotions any longer. Regrets nagged, getting their hooks in and clawing their way to the surface, attacking her from different angles. The first one was for bringing David into this, for involving him in her life in a chase that had ended up injuring him. That was the guilt that had glowed the brightest today, but focusing on that one had covered another. She regretted opening this wound inside them, the wound of their past that had healed, at least on the surface, at least enough for them to move on and continue with life. Now hers was open, raw, chafing, hurting in ways she couldn't even predict. But as she skied over Isabel's snowmobile tracks, laid out and glittering in the night, she knew the regret that ran deeper, however painful it was to admit.

She regretted leaving David.

The thought struck her like thunder, rattling her insides. Maybe it had been there all along, lurking, wanting, but she had so successfully kept it buried that she had never once, even in those lowest days when she missed him, thought she'd made the wrong choice. She had always believed that she had done them both a favor, an excruciating but necessary choice to protect both of them. The fighting about his job would end. Every day when he walked into his job, she would no longer stay up, wondering if he might never come back.

It was a strange and unsettling regret. Even if she somehow could go back five years and tell herself about it, she wasn't sure if she would've believed it. But all she could think about now was the chance they had missed. Maybe, if she hadn't left him, they would be sitting by the fire in his cabin, tucked in as the snow fell outdoors.

She had given up the man she loved, and after a while, it had gotten easier. After a while, she no longer found herself pacing, waiting for his car, waiting to hear his voice to let her know he had made it through another day. There had been enough relief that she had believed the choice was right.

But as the noise of Isabel's snowmobile faded, she found herself playing out the worst-case scenario.

The thought that rang loudest through her mind was this: *if David dies, I will have missed his last five years on earth.* After years of efforts to distance herself, it struck her hard that she would have missed all the happiness it could have brought, to both of them. The idea of him dying was no less devastating. Shouldn't this distance have lessened the blow somehow?

And yet, the fear for what could happen to him was enough to break her completely. The only thing keeping her on her feet was the knowledge that Isabel might need her help, that she had promised him to be there when he woke up. If he woke up.

A flame deep down flickered and sparked. The strength she had found to face the attacker alone was still there, coming from within, helping her forward. She had always tried to trust God's path, but how could she not have doubts when she had seen so much loss? As uncertainty stretched out in front of her, she went over the last day, the moments she and David had together. If it was David's time, if that was the path that God had decided for him, she was grateful she'd at least been part of that path at the end.

Though her regret still weighed heavily, that hope sparked brighter. *You don't know God's plan. All you have is this moment, right now. Do the best you can with it.*

The strength inside her was burning brighter, releasing some of the burden of her remorse with its energy. This was the feeling she was searching for when she stood on Crystal Ridge, trying to find a way to say goodbye to Brandon. It wasn't the past or a pursuit of truth that she needed to let go of—it was fear. So strange that she was finding this now, when David had disappeared into the night, into an uncertain future, when she was teetering on the precipice of another loss. But the feeling was there, glowing inside her. It wasn't happiness, not quite. It felt more like freedom.

Rain's skis glided smoothly, and soon she passed the switchback where she had stopped. She went farther, skiing faster as love for David blazed inside her. The sound of rushing water got clearer and clearer. She was nearing the river, nearing the bridge that she needed to cross to get to Clover Valley. She pulled out David's phone and tapped in his passcode, but she couldn't get a signal.

Trust in God's path.

She tried a few more times on the way to Clover Valley Urgent Care, but she couldn't get through. She skied through the quiet Main Street and into the semicircular drive of the clinic. The Hernandezes' snowmobile was parked in front of the double doors. Rain ditched her skis and ran inside.

"The man that came in on the snowmobile," she said, trying to keep the impatience out of her voice. "Is...is he still alive?"

She stood in the empty waiting room, the fluorescent lights glaring down at her, panting. The man behind the glass frowned.

"Are you a family member of one of our patients?"

"He's not family. He's just…" She closed her eyes and shook her head. "He's just someone I love."

When she opened her eyes, the man's expression had softened. "I'm sorry, ma'am, but patient information is private."

Rain's whole body sagged. Of course they couldn't disclose anything. Still, she had hoped for…well, some sort of clue. The rush of the day hit her hard, and she itched to do something. But all she could do was take a deep breath and bite back her frustration.

"I'll just wait." Rain bit her lip. "But can I use your phone?"

The man nodded, and she lifted the receiver and dialed 911. After reporting the stash of guns and the man on the road, Rain hung up the phone and clomped away, her outerwear bulky and uncomfortable in the warmth of the indoors. She took off her pack and sank into one of the maroon waiting room chairs. She pulled off her gloves and stared at the television screen flickering in front of her. The news was playing on mute, showing scenes of fallen trees and treacherous freeways. She looked away and unzipped her jacket, comforting herself that the snowmobile parked outside meant that Isabel and David had made it here. At some point, they'd have to come out this way. All she could do was wait. And pray.

She didn't know how much time passed in that

empty waiting room, under the harsh glow of the lights. It could have been minutes, or it could have been hours. Then, she heard the squeak of boots on the hallway floor, the swoosh of the double doors that led to the clinic's rooms, and Isabel appeared. Rain jumped to her feet.

"Is he okay?" Rain's voice was a rasp, barely there, as if speaking these words softly might lessen her fear. It didn't.

"He's not…awake right now." Isabel's lips trembled. "But they're treating him for hypothermia, giving him blood, and the doctor sewed up the wound. She said he was lucky to have you around."

Isabel frowned as she said that last part, as if she wasn't sure whether she had the same view of the situation. Rain was inclined to agree with her.

Rain didn't remember starting to move, but she somehow had made her way across and was standing in front of Isabel. Rain opened her arms and wrapped them around her old friend, one that she had lost along the way. The least she could do was offer comfort. Isabel stilled, as if this were the last thing she'd expected. She took a breath, then another, and finally she laid her head on Rain's shoulder and let out a quiet sob.

"I'm so, so sorry," whispered Rain. "For everything."

David woke up alone in a small hospital room. An IV was attached to his arm and a pulse oxymeter pinched his finger. Both were connected to a monitor at the side of his bed, drawing his heartbeats in steady peaks. How long had he been out? The window looked out into the dark landscape, and the snow and trees were lit by the lights from the street. The corridor outside his room was quiet.

David searched his memories for clues, but they were hazy at best. All he remembered were fragments of images, noises, sensations—they faded in and out, sometimes just wisps he tried to hang on to, and sometimes in bursts, all at once. He remembered the burn of pain in his arm, and the drone of the snowmobile, the sound of Isabel's voice telling him to try to hold on. It was just so hard to stay awake.

Where had Rain been in all this? Those details came back, fuzzy. He recalled begging her not to leave him until this was over. Or maybe he had just thought those words. Whether he had pleaded with her in memory or imagination, Rain had answered. She had told him she wouldn't leave him, and that knowledge had kept him going. The last blur of his memory was of being lifted onto the gurney outside the hospital from the snowmobile. As he faded off into darkness, it had occurred to him that only one regret remained. He shouldn't have held back. He should have told Rain that he loved her.

Rain had promised to stay until he woke up, hadn't she? Yes, that memory was too sharp, too painful to be a dream. It wasn't fair of him to ask that of her, but then again, nothing about this situation in the last two days had been fair.

David lifted his arm experimentally. There was the feeling that he'd gotten run over by a snowplow or two. He had carried one hundred pounds of equipment through the mountains all day for a week straight, yet that was nothing compared to the bone-deep exhaustion of this moment. The shuttering and shivering came through from his hazy memories. Where was Isabel? Had Rain made it here? This question found its way to the front of his mind. That and his craving for a sip of water.

He searched the various cords and mechanisms around his bed until he found the call button. He pressed it, and the red light on the wall lit up. A few moments later, someone in scrubs appeared at his doorway.

"Mr. Hernandez. It's good to see you awake," the man said.

"I'm glad to be awake." His voice came out harsh, scratchy. "May I have a glass of water?"

"Of course. I'd like to do a check of your vital signs, and then I'll let your sister know that you're awake."

"Thank you."

Isabel and he had always been close, and it was a comfort to know she was near. One of the reasons he was able to go out and do the work he did was because he knew, without a doubt, that his family would always be there for him. But right now, it wasn't his sister that he needed to see. Isabel would kill him if she knew this, but he had the rest of his life to talk with her. What he wanted was a few minutes alone with Rain. The last time things had gone so badly between them, his pride was wounded and he'd been blindsided by her betrayal of leaving him. If these were their last moments, he wanted to make sure he did it right this time. He wanted to tell her the things he wished he had said that day. This wouldn't change their path together, but it made a difference in the way he lived his life.

It occurred to him that he trusted that Rain was here. He could feel it when she'd said so. Logic— and the last five years—told him to be wary, but his heart soared anyway. When she had told him she loved him, he had felt it deep inside. Maybe it would be enough to start something new, or maybe it wouldn't. All he could do was trust himself and trust their path.

Which meant he needed to figure out how to get his sister to let Rain in the room and leave them alone for a few minutes.

David was poked and prodded, and then, soon after, Isabel rushed through the door. She rushed to his bedside and enveloped him in a hug. He winced as she accidentally pressed against his arm, but he didn't move away. What he felt most in that moment was grateful—grateful that his sister was there to prop him up when he couldn't stand on his own. His whole family was. It was what Rain had lost. The thought hit him, just as hard as it had all those years ago.

Rain. When he looked up, she was standing in the doorway. She looked down at the floor, then met his gaze again, as if she wasn't sure what she should say or if she should even be there.

"You're awake," his sister said to him in rapid Spanish. "The doctor said that the wound looked okay, all things considered. The bullet didn't hit the bone, so you got stitches and antibiotics, but she wasn't sure…" Isabel's voice wavered. "She wasn't sure how long it would take for you to wake up."

"I feel pretty good. Just tired." He tried to sound upbeat for his sister's sake, but she frowned.

"You need food. And not the food they have here."

At the word food, David's stomach gave a hollow tug. Yes, he definitely needed food, and he was inclined to agree with his sister. The place was far too small for anything more than prepackaged meals, heated in a little microwave. Though right now he might just be hungry enough to stomach one of those…

"I didn't want to leave before you woke up, but you should be eating my cooking. I'm taking a quick trip to the cabin. That will give you two a few minutes to say whatever…" Isabel let the sentence drift off, motioning between them. She left off the last part of her sentence, but he was sure Rain heard the implication as well as he did. She was giving them space to say goodbye. Isabel glanced in Rain's direction, and his sister's pointed gaze made him wonder if this was some sort of compromise they had discussed before they came in.

His sister gave him one more hug, then said, "I'll be back soon with decent food."

She disappeared out the door, leaving him alone in the bland little room with Rain. Isabel's footsteps faded down the hallway, and he heard the swoosh of the sliding door. Neither he nor Rain spoke, just looked at each other. There was a softness in her eyes, a tenderness that hit him hard. It would almost be better if she were exuding anger or hurt or something other than this warmth. Once again, he was struck by how helpless this woman could make him feel. He had given everything to her, and she had still turned away. But if this were the path that God had chosen for him, he was ready to accept it. This time, he wouldn't call her selfish or try to hurt her the way she had hurt him. He would let her know how he felt, then let her walk away.

"I guess it's just the two of us for a while," he said, breaking the silence. "Where is the guy who was chasing you?"

"I called the police, and they were sending someone up to get him."

"Did you get in touch with the police?"

Rain nodded. "As soon as I got cell reception. Someone from ATF is coming in as soon as they dig out Route 80. The snow has mostly stopped, so that should be soon." She paused, then added, "They're picking me up here at the hospital so I can give them all the details."

A little of his tension had left as she described how she and Isabel had handled the situation, but that was quickly replaced by a familiar sinking feeling the moment she mentioned that she was leaving him again. This would never be easy, no matter how it happened. Rain had always had the power to make him feel things he didn't feel with anyone else. He longed to rise out of bed and hold her, comfort her. But all he had was words, words that he hadn't gotten right before. He had to get them right this time.

"Before you go, I just wanted to say a few things. That I'm sorry for the way things ended between us. I'm sorry I called you selfish five years ago. But most of all, I'm sorry I didn't tell you I love you after you said that to me up on the mountain. If I hadn't made it, you would never have heard it from me one last time."

Rain took a few steps closer to his bed. Her bottom lip was trembling. She walked across the room and sat down on the bed next to him. Her hands rested on top of his. Did he trust this moment? Did he trust the words she'd said on the mountain? He turned his hand over so they were palm against palm.

Then he took a chance. He closed his fingers around her hands. She smiled the way he hadn't seen in a long, long time.

"After you and Isabel took off, I had a long time by myself, to think," she said quietly. Strength and determination radiated from her as she looked into his eyes. "I thought a lot about Brandon, too. About the way it had never occurred to me that God might take him. All that time I'd spent thinking about that part, even…" She paused, swallowed. "Even getting angry at the world, angry with God for taking him. But as I was out there, alone in the night, it really hit me that He *hadn't* taken you. I left you because of that risk, and nothing went the way I thought it would. And in the end, I missed these last five years with you."

David's heart was beating faster as that stubborn flame of hope inside him blazed higher.

Her cheeks reddened, and she gave a little laugh. "I promised myself I'd tell you this if…if I made it in time, but it's harder than I thought it would be. It's hard to admit I was so wrong. All those years we spent apart, all those ways that I hurt you, and I was wrong. I didn't care about you any less because I distanced myself. I just missed out on being with you."

David should have felt a triumph of relief, but this happiness wouldn't last. Even if his trust in her could mend, the wedge between them was still there.

"You weren't wrong to protect yourself," he said.

"We both could've said things differently, left things differently, but in the end, the problem is still there."

She shook her head. "But that's what I realized. Don't you see? I thought that I could protect myself from hurt, and it meant I couldn't give myself a chance for happiness. The kind of happiness I feel when I'm with you."

Maybe he was still a little groggy, because this was starting to sound less and less like a goodbye. But the problems hadn't gone away. If anything, the last two days had only made them more apparent.

"My job hasn't gotten any less dangerous," he said. "I'll be laid up for a bit while my arm heals, but after that…"

He didn't finish his sentence, but he didn't have to. She knew what it meant for him to be on duty for stretches of days. During the summers, those days stretched into weeks if the firefighters were far enough into the wilderness. David could give her concessions, list the things he wasn't going to do, but in the end, that didn't take away the problem. His job was dangerous, and he loved it. It was just as much a part of him as she was.

But she wasn't frowning the way she always had when they talked about this years ago. In fact, her expression remained as resolute as ever.

"I say all the time to myself that I don't know God's plan, so why should I pretend to know it for you?" she said. "I spent so much energy, caused so much pain when I tried to steer our paths so I wouldn't get hurt. But I did get hurt. Blindsided. And so as I skied here, all alone, I promised myself that I wouldn't do that anymore. That I would make my decisions from the heart." She met his gaze and whispered, "With love."

"I see," he said.

It wasn't the most articulate of responses, but he was having a hard time processing all of this. Before he could formulate something better, she spoke again.

"Of course I know that this isn't a given. I know that just because I'm seeing this in a new way doesn't mean that you should, too. But I just wanted to tell you—"

"I do want to try, Rain," he said. "But you left me without even a discussion. How do I know that won't happen again?"

She lowered her eyes. "I can promise you I won't do that again. All I can do is try to earn back your trust, but I understand that will take time."

He swallowed. It all came down to trust. Could he take that leap and try to trust her again?

"Just tell me what you need. I want to figure this out. With you." She squeezed his hand.

He had always liked her hands—strong, capable. She saved lives with these hands, his included. Her hand was the connection he had wanted for too long. Somehow, the wall of their past seemed smaller as their connection grew. Not gone but smaller. It wasn't the same as before, not quite. Their bond had been battered, but he knew that they could build it back, stronger than before.

They sat there, holding hands, David remembering how it was to just be together. He didn't notice the man standing at the door of his room until he knocked on the open door.

"Rain Jordan?"

Rain let go of his hand, breaking their newfound connection, and stood up. "Yes, that's me."

The man flashed his badge. "I'm Ravi Chand. I have a crew waiting outside. Are you ready?"

She glanced back at David, and he nodded. "We'll finish this later."

Rain turned to Ravi and followed him out the door. He was surprised that fear didn't come for him as he watched her walk away. This was part of their path. He was going to trust that they were meant to be together.

Chapter Fifteen

⁓

The next two days passed in a blur, between Rain's visits to the hospital and the time she spent with the agent from the Bureau of Alcohol, Tobacco, Firearms and Explosives, trying to untangle the mess Brandon had created. Once the storm had safely passed, she led a ski expedition to the cookout ledge, where the weapons were, indeed, stashed. She and Maple watched from Crystal Ridge as the helicopter lifted out the box the agents had transferred the weapons into, wanting to see with her own eyes that they were gone. That this was over.

On the way home that first night, the police had found the attacker on the side of the road and his wife and their baby in the trailer, waiting for him. Rain had wanted some sort of guarantee that justice would be served to that man who had taken her brother's life. Justice, however imperfect, was a comfort. It helped to see that fairness still existed, even when she faced the pain of loss and uncertainty. She knew that finding one shipment and arresting one person in the delivery chain hadn't solved the whole problem, but she was relieved that she and David had made some sort of difference in the trafficking of illegal guns into California.

Maple had been overjoyed when Rain had picked her up late that first night, licking her face and jumping up on her. Since then, the dog had stuck closer than usual. Rain had left her alone when she'd gone to work, but somehow Maple seemed to feel that this recent experience was different. It definitely had been for Rain. She'd spent a little extra time on the sofa, cuddling with Maple and letting her twisted ankle rest.

The agent had left, so today's project was to patch up the windows that their attacker had shot through. Rain had put up some plastic, but she still had needed her winter coat around her cabin for the last two days.

She was thankful the Hernandez family had extra plywood sitting in their garage from some renovations, and Isabel had offered to help her nail it over the broken windows. Rain was pretty sure David had pressured his sister to help. He could ask for anything from his family while he was in the hospital, and they wouldn't say no. Even if they didn't particularly like the task. Rain couldn't afford to turn down the offer, either. Getting someone to replace the windows would take weeks. She was grateful at least Maple was there to break the tension when Isabel came over.

"Do you want to hammer first or do you want to hold up the plywood?" she asked Isabel as she picked up the wood.

"I'll hammer," said Isabel.

Rain placed the thick plywood over the front window, and Isabel held up the other end, lining it up with the casing. They worked side by side in silence, fixing the window as Maple watched from her bed in the middle of the rug, ears perked.

She and Isabel hadn't spoken much over the last couple of days beyond the practicalities of David's stay at the clinic and the logistics of the windows. They had taken turns keeping David company and bringing him food as he healed. In better weather conditions, he might have been discharged, but the trip up the mountain on a snowmobile had been a stretch, so the medical staff had kept him an extra day. Each time Isabel arrived, Rain had been careful to leave quickly, and Isabel had done nothing to discourage that. She wasn't impolite, and Rain knew that Isabel would never leave her in her need. She had known this for sure the day Isabel and her mother had shown up at Brandon's funeral. Although Rain had hurt David, and despite the protectiveness their family felt for each other, they would still help her. It was one of the things she had loved about the

Hernandezes—their hearts were large enough for more than just the four of them. It meant that David's parents lived with David and Isabel's aunt when she became a widow and helped raise her son. It was why Rain had felt the embrace of his family so deeply when she had lost her own parents.

When she left David, she had known the ache of missing him would be strong in the short term. But Rain hadn't fully registered how much she'd miss his family, too. As she worked beside Isabel, she felt that loss most acutely.

"Any updates on the woman and child in the trailer? Are they still there?" Isabel asked.

Rain had been in daily contact with the team.

"They're going in for questioning when the plow comes in," said Rain. "All of Crystal Lake has the Bureau to thank for getting the plows up here so quickly."

Usually, Crystal Lake was the last priority when it came to plowing, with its long mountain road and so few residents.

Isabel let out a little laugh. "That's looking at the bright side of things."

"I'm working on that."

She was, truly. It was going to take a lot of practice, after years of clinging to worst-case scenarios. Maybe it was natural after all the tragedy she'd experienced, but she didn't have to live like that. Since that night she had found David in the emergency room, she had been trying, but it was a harder habit to break than she'd imagined. Prayer helped, and so had the conversations she'd had with David when they'd just focused on their moments together. She was starting to think she might add counseling into that mix, too. It was a long road, but she was more determined than ever to do it. For her, for David, and for the possibility of a life together.

But since that first night, they hadn't talked about the future. Hours passed as she sat by his bedside, catching up on the last five years, listening to the things he had done on his job. This was new. Before, she had been too frightened to ask for the details, and he had known better than to tell her. Now she tried to open herself to them. And every time she felt the fear rising, she had whispered, *Thank You, God, for letting David survive that.* David had repeated the prayerful thanks, smiling. These were baby steps. As much as she loved sitting and talking to him, it was hard to see him in the clinic, with the nurses and assistance coming in to check up on him. It felt as if they were hanging in limbo, with his heartbeat ticking away on the monitor.

He was coming home, so things were about to change. It would no longer be only the two of them, alone in that little room. His whole family was going to be there. What would happen if his family couldn't forgive her? David's family was at the center of his life. Could they trust and accept a woman who had broken his heart?

"Your parents must be aching to see David," she said, breaking the silence.

Isabel had had to talk them out of immediately driving up from Sacramento. Aside from the treacherous highway driving during the snowstorm, they wouldn't have had anywhere to stay once they arrived until the snowplow came through. They were willing to sleep in chairs in the hospital room, but David had vetoed their attempt.

"My parents should be up here by noon," said Isabel, taking another nail from her tool belt. "They're planning to pick up David and then follow the plow in. Literally."

Rain grinned. She could see that. She glanced at Isabel.

"David invited me over this afternoon, but I don't know if that's a good idea."

Isabel paused, then continued to hammer without comment.

"I know your family would never kick me out," Rain continued, "but I want to be respectful. I hurt you all, and I'm so sorry for that. I was just so afraid. People do stupid things to protect themselves when they're afraid." She swallowed and added, "And by 'people' I mean me."

Isabel let the hammer fall to her side and turned to face Rain. It felt like the first time that day that Isabel had looked her right in the eyes.

"You know he signs up for the danger on his own. My parents understand that, and...and maybe I am starting to as well." Isabel rested a hand on Rain's arm. "I guess what I'm trying to say is you should come over this afternoon. Not just for David. For all of us."

Rain bit her lip, trying to hold back the rays of hope bursting from somewhere deep inside her. Maple jumped out of her bed and ran across the room, pacing between them, her tail whacking Rain in the thigh.

"As soon as when we finish hammering, I think we need a group hug," she said, and Isabel laughed.

That little flame of hope was getting bigger.

They fixed the windows and played with Maple out in the snow. Then it was time for Isabel to go back to the Hernandez cabin.

"When you come over, bring Maple so my parents can meet her," she said as she headed off on her skis.

Rain was going to drive herself crazy, staring out the window and watching for David and his parents to arrive, so she busied herself with all the chores she still hadn't done. She cleared a path along the short driveway and a little trail to her front porch. It was one of those side benefits of all this stress energy, but the cabin was spotless, aside from Brandon's room. After the events of the last few days, she needed a little more time before she went through it.

As the morning turned to afternoon, and she still hadn't heard from David, she took down her mother's old cookbook and found a recipe for browned-butter chocolate chip cookies. Soon, the cabin smelled like butter and sugar and chocolate. As she pulled the first baking tray out of the oven, the plow rumbled by, followed by the engine of a car not long after. Rain ran to the window, watching the car drive by, her heart thumping, but she forced herself to stay in the cabin, to give them a little time. Minutes dragged by, the sun falling behind the mountains, and finally her phone dinged.

Want to stop by our cabin?

Just a few mundane words, but they lifted her. She stuffed the cookies into her backpack and then called to Maple as she stood next to the front door. "Time to go out."

Her dog sprinted to her, tail wagging, her claws scratching over the wooden surface of the floor. Rain hoped Maple would act as an emissary, since Rain was unsure of what kind of reception the Hernandez family would give her. At this point, she needed all the help she could get.

The sky was blue, and the sun shone down on the snow, sparkling and bright. The day was peaceful, with only the sound of the wind in the trees. A snowblower started, echoing across the lake, then stopped. Rain breathed in the cold, crisp air as she skied up the newly formed bank and glided down onto the road. Maple followed her, bouncing along the packed snow. When the Hernandez cabin came into view, her heart thumped harder in her chest. The log cabin–style house shone against white clouds of snow surrounding it. Someone had used the snow-blower to clear a path to the door, probably Isabel, considering the condition of David's arm. She skied up to the front porch and propped her equipment against the enormous snowbank next to the porch. She inspected Maple's paws for snow clumps, then walked up the steps.

"We need to make our best impression," she said. "Try not to scare little Fifi."

Maple licked her face in response, and Rain lifted her lips. "Things work out, just not in the way you expect, right, girl?"

In some ways it wasn't that simple. Rain had suffered so much loss, more than she thought she could handle some days. Yet, as she approached the front door, her heart was full. She took a deep breath, staring at the front of the cabin. Was it just three days ago that she had stood here? So much had changed in so little time. Then again, there were things, important things, that hadn't changed in five years. Like the fact that she loved David. She was going to trust that love, lean into it, even knowing that it might not last.

Rain straightened, took a deep breath and knocked.

David stood in the front hallway, pacing back and forth. Tía Maribel had spotted Rain skiing down the road from the second-story window, and his family had agreed to stay in the kitchen until he'd had a chance to talk with her. The truth was, though things were going well, and though Rain had told him more than once that she loved him, he remained uneasy. Somewhere in the back of his mind, he wondered if she was coming to say goodbye. Nothing she had said suggested she would, but this feeling wasn't rational, and it didn't respond to logic. The remnants of their past lingered inside him, so he told himself that if she defied those worst-case expectations, if she came to the door today still ready to start anew, he would need to leave those remnants in the past. If they were going to have a chance, they needed to start fresh, him included.

Minute after minute stretched out as he waited, but finally, she knocked. David rested his hand on the door handle, blew out a breath and opened the door.

Rain stood in front of him, beautiful as always. Her cheeks were pink from the cold and the exercise, and snowflakes covered her hat. Her brown eyes were warm, but she gave him an uncertain lift of her lips. Maple wandered in, and Fifi barked from somewhere in the kitchen. Rain held on to her collar, Maple dragging her inside.

"Hi." Her voice was soft, tentative. "How's your arm?"

He gestured to his left arm. "It's okay. They wanted me to put it in a sling, mostly so I didn't move it too much these first days."

He met her gaze and held it. *Have faith. Trust the path you're on.*

"I should probably dry off her paws before she comes in any farther," she said.

David stepped out of the way, and Rain entered. It took both of them to dry off Maple as the dog yipped, her attention focused on the direction of the kitchen. When she was dry, or at least dryer, he called to Isabel.

"Are you ready for another dog?"

"Of course."

Rain told Maple to lie down and looked her in the eye.

"Take it easy, girl," she said with a chuckle.

Maple wagged her tail but stayed put.

"All right, you can go." Her dog scrambled up and started for the kitchen, leaving them alone in the little hallway.

"Are you sure this is okay?" Rain asked.

David laughed. "Isabel has been talking about that dog all afternoon to my parents."

Rain gave him a little smile. "I meant for me."

David had known she wasn't just talking about the dog. "My parents want to see you, but I wanted a few minutes with you first, before we go in."

She furrowed her brow a little, like she was just as uncertain about this as he was. That was why he needed to lay things out for her, clearly. No matter how it went, at least he would have made his feelings clear this time. If it didn't work, it wasn't going to be because he hadn't tried. That was all he could do. Try his best. The rest he'd leave to God.

"I've had a lot of time to think over the last few days," he said. "Not much else to do in that hospital bed."

She smiled a little, but the worried look stayed on her face.

"I want us to have a new chance, but I don't know quite what that looks like. Things are different between us, but my feelings haven't changed. I love you in a way I don't think I could love anyone else. I want us to be together. And I can take it slow, get used to being together, but I want to be clear about where I want this to go. In my mind, there's no halfway with us." The words spilled out of him, like five years of feelings set free. The more he said, the more he knew this was the right thing to do. "I don't know what to do about my job. I've become more careful since Hakeem passed, but in the end, my job is still dangerous. Nothing is going to change that. And I want to know where you stand in all of this."

As he spoke, the lines on her brow disappeared. In fact, she was smiling.

"Did you just ask me to be your girlfriend again, David Hernandez?"

David's heart gave a strange jolt, and he swiped a hand over his face. "I suppose I did."

"Then yes," she said. "I'd love to start again with you."

He looked at her. "I don't have any solutions yet. This was just…"

"Incredibly romantic?" she filled in.

"I'm glad you see it that way." He was trying to rein in the feelings that were soaring inside. He needed to say the things that were hardest, if they were going to move on. "But we could be like Hakeem and Angela. You know better than anyone that things don't always end happily."

She lifted her hand and stroked his cheek. Her touch was light and her eyes were soft, like she was weighing what he'd said. She gave him a little grin. "Even if something happened to you, we would have had time together. Do you think Angela regrets the time she had with Hakeem?"

David shook his head.

"I've already tried to live without you," she whispered. "I want these moments, this feeling between us, even if it comes without guarantees."

Rain found his hand and laced her fingers with his.

"I love you, David, and I want you to be a part of my life for however long our lives may be. That's what I didn't understand the last time. That's what's important. And there probably will be times that I will worry, but I choose love over fear." She let out a little laugh. "It's a work in progress."

She was wearing her jacket, wet from the snow, but she reached for him and hugged him, and it felt like coming home. She looked up, and he lowered his lips to hers, kissing her deeply. This was the man she wanted to spend the rest of her life with. He looked into her eyes, and they stood there, just seeing each other. She could have stayed there holding him.

Maple found her way into the hallway with Fifi following in her trail. The dogs nosed them and raced around the entryway until they finally let go and reached out to pet them.

"Are you ready for the full force of my family?" he asked.

"I can't think of anything I'd like better." She let go of his hand and unzipped her backpack, pulling out the glass jar full of cookies. "Ready."

"Mamá? Papá? Tía Maribel?"

Footsteps clattered across the living room, and then his family was there, crowding into the little hallway, talking and laughing and taking turns hugging her. And with each hug, with each welcoming smile, Rain's heart soared with happiness. She belonged here with his family. They belonged together.

* * * * *

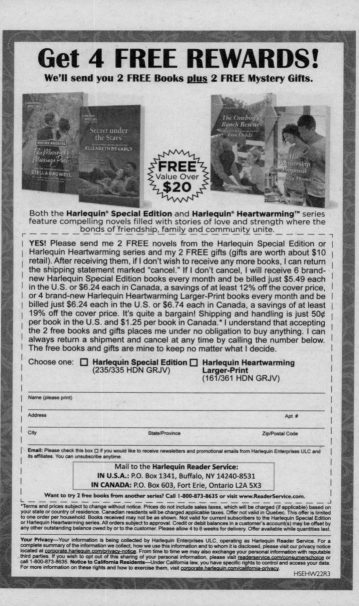

HARLEQUIN
PLUS

Try the best multimedia
subscription service for romance
readers like you!

Read, Watch and Play.

Experience the easiest way to get
the romance content you crave.

Start your **FREE TRIAL** at
<u>www.harlequinplus.com/freetrial</u>.